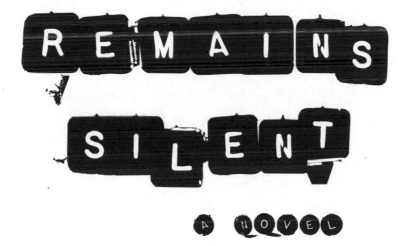

REMAINS SILENT

A NOVEL

MICHAEL BADEN & LINDA KENNEY

ALFRED A. KNOPF   NEW YORK   2005

THIS IS A BORZOI BOOK
PUBLISHED BY ALFRED A. KNOPF

Knopf, Borzoi Books, and the colophon are registered
trademarks of Random House, Inc.

Library of Congress Cataloging-in-Publication Data
Baden, Michael M.
Remains silent : a novel / Michael Baden & Linda Kenney.— 1st ed.
    p.   cm.
"This is a Borzoi book."
ISBN 1-4000-4419-7
1. Women lawyers—Fiction.   2. Forensic pathologists—Fiction.
3. New York (State)—Fiction.   I. Kenney, Linda, 1953–   II. Title.
PS3602.A358R46 2005
813'.6—dc22   2005015783

Printed in the United States of America
First Edition

LK: In memoriam to my father, Benjamin Benincasa, and to the real Filomena Manfreda, my mother, Faye Benincasa.

MB: To Eli and Ruby, our future.

No man chooses evil because it is evil;
he only mistakes it for happiness, the good he seeks.

—Mary Wollstonecraft Godwin Shelley

PROLOGUE

THERE WERE LOTS of things that drove her nuts: crowds, waiting in line, cheap shoes, lawyers without ethics—but at the top of the list was being late for court. Manny *hated* it, absolutely hated it.

If she got to the courthouse looking like an escaped mental patient, as she sometimes did, she took time to pull herself together. No way she'd appear before a judge unless she was the quintessence of cool. After a visit to the ladies' room, her makeup would be flawless; every strand of flaming red hair would be in place. The line of her smooth stockings would lead to the very latest Vecchio stiletto heels; her documents would be in order, her arguments honed and ready for attack. At the very least, she would have earrings in both ears. She believed that an impeccable appearance bespeaks an orderly mind.

But timeliness and impeccable appearance might not be possible today. No, on this unexpectedly sweltering first Thursday in September, Manny was late and she was a mess.

It wasn't really her fault. Her sports car should have started even though she'd left the vanity light on all night; an empty cab should have been available in front of her office, even though it was rush hour. Her fellow passengers herded onto the PATH commuter train should have given her room, even though there was not an extra inch of space and the man behind her seemed to enjoy pushing up against her butt. When without explanation the train stopped short of her station and sat in the tunnel for ten minutes, when she discovered she had somehow somewhere lost an earring, when the train finally lurched forward and the man stepped on her heel—no wonder she was sweating, agitated, and thoroughly pissed off when she got to Newark. Not the best frame of mind for arguing a high-profile civil rights case before a jury and a federal judge, a case close to her heart, one she was determined to win.

Manny didn't like people to be treated unfairly; it was as simple as that. Her attitude started early. As a teenager, Manny and her best friend Leigh applied for summer jobs at a new doughnut shop on Main Street. Manny was hired. But Leigh, who was black, was not. Injustice! screamed Manny's soul. She vowed to fight, and fight she did. She organized a boycott of the shop, demonstrated in front of it with posters that accused the owners of racist hiring practices, and got the local television station to run a segment about it on the evening news. And she got a better job. Manny and Leigh were both hired as counselors at the local community center by the director, who was impressed by her activism.

Now, five years out of law school, Manny had earned a reputation as a tenacious fighter for the underdog. She had taken and won cases for the socially disadvantaged and disenfranchised, the kind of clients white-bread law firms considered beneath them. Lawyers wearing Brooks Brothers suits and club ties didn't relate well to clients in baggy jeans with tattoos and body piercing, though she—even in Dolce & Gabbana and Versace—had the knack. Besides, Manny's clients couldn't afford to pay $600 an hour. Often they paid little or nothing. If she won their cases, she took a percentage of the awards.

Manny was prepared to raise hell again, this time at the wrongful-death trial of Esmeralda Carramia. As she waited to go through the metal detectors, she regained her composure, for she had enough time to freshen up before court resumed—less than ten minutes, but enough. She was ready. She knew the case inside and out, having memorized the facts so thoroughly she might as well have been at the crime scene herself. The events central to the Carramia case had unfolded in a matter of minutes, but it was enough time to leave a family heartbroken, a city torn apart, and a police force accused of racism and brutality.

Newark, New Jersey, November 25, 2003. Esmeralda Carramia walks into Steinless, the last department store left downtown. She needs a birthday present for her grandmother. Esmeralda, her grandmother's adored Essie, is the daughter of emigrants from the Dominican Republic who have just moved from Miami to Newark. The store clerk, who is white, pointedly ignores her. Then she accuses Essie of shoplifting a $49 silk scarf. Essie denies it. Voices are raised. Security is called. Essie gets agitated. She is told to calm down. She does not. The police arrive within minutes. Essie's tote bag is searched; a scarf is found, price tag dangling. She says the clerk planted it there, swears it on the Virgin of Guadalupe. No one believes her. The police take her outside, try to arrest her. Essie resists. She lashes out. Her parents will testify this is completely out of character. In the mêlée, one officer takes a knee to the groin; another's nose is bloodied. Backup arrives. By now there are six policemen on the sidewalk, none weighing less than 160 pounds. Essie, at 5 feet 2 inches, weighs 105.

Later, no one can say who was responsible when her head struck the pavement. As the police put her in the squad car, they realize she is unconscious. At the hospital, Esmeralda Carramia is declared brain dead. She is nineteen years old.

Injustice!

Manny had taken the case two months later, when Esmeralda's parents arrived in her office armed with childhood pictures and righteous indignation. They had come to America for a better life, they said, and the people sworn to protect Essie had murdered her instead. Here was a picture of Essie dressed in white for her first communion, and in a white frilly gown for her *quinceañera*. And if Manny needed further convincing, here on their lap was little Amaryllis—their one-year-old granddaughter, Essie's daughter—destined to grow up without a mother.

Though no amount of money would bring their daughter back, they wanted the people who killed her to pay.

Manny had jumped into the case with her usual zeal. She had deposed the cops, the witnesses, and the store employees. There was no question as to the facts: Esmeralda had struggled, fallen, and died. Her forensic pathologist had agreed with the state medical examiner on the cause of Essie's death: a blow to the head resulting in a subdural hemorrhage.

Essie's parents and grandmother had been simple and eloquent in their testimony. Their Essie was a good girl, religious, never done anything wrong before, let alone stealing. Manny had rested her case, knowing the jury's sympathy was with her clients. Let opposing counsel try to justify the cops' actions. She would use whatever they said to rip them apart in her closing argument.

When Manny went through the metal detectors, an alarm beeped. The federal marshal waved a wand down the length of her body, stopping at her shoes: Italian designer black-on-black fabric-embroidered d'Orsay pumps. "You gotta stop wearing these, Ms. M," he said. "I've told you a thousand times, there's metal in the heels."

"Just testing you," Manny said flirtatiously. "Besides, they go with my outfit." She walked across the green-and-white marble floor of the courthouse's imposing rotunda and headed upstairs to the ladies' room.

Manny fixed her makeup, put her hair up in a twist, and smoothed the jacket and skirt of her electric-blue suit with the leopard skin lining. The suit brought out the color of her steel blue eyes, and the matching V-necked silk blouse offered a little something to keep the male jurors happy. Not too bad, she thought, assessing herself in the mirror. I can pass off the one-earring look as a fashion statement.

At twenty-nine, she knew that some of her colleagues thought she wore killer shoes and bright colors to make herself stand out—but that wasn't totally accurate. Her clothes were a kind of armor, a talisman. They declared she was someone who made bold decisions and was confident and comfortable with herself. Your clothes not only represent who you are, they also say what you *want* to be. When she became a trial lawyer, the philosophy served her well. She knew instinctively that juries would be more inclined to believe a well-dressed, smartly accessorized lawyer than a woman trying to look like a man in a bow tie, boring low-heeled black shoes, and a shapeless suit. Her parents had taught her to buy the best clothing she could afford, even if it meant eating bean soup for dinner. Even now there was soup many nights, but she ate it, if alone, in a Ralph Lauren bathrobe. Her family was proud of her. And she liked to shop, especially sales. It was her primary hobby.

She examined herself in the mirror one last time, aware of her flaws—owing to her healthy appetite for food and wine and her 5-feet-8-inch height, she wore a size eight rather than the four she fantasized; also, there was a little bump at the edge of her nose, a genetic inheritance from her father she hadn't had the nerve to fix with plastic surgery—but reasonably satisfied. Her cheekbones were good—she got *those* from her mother—and the fire in her eyes, the joy of battle, was hers alone.

A stranger in the courtroom might assume she was someone's client—another society wife—a lady who lunched. An opposing lawyer might treat her as a bimbo who was sleeping with one of the senior partners—until she presented her case, that is.

Manny had remembered to pin a small square of red cloth inside her suit jacket for luck, something her grandmother had taught her to do, just in case. She was taking no chances; no one would cast an evil eye on her, not today. She needed to win.

She entered the courtroom—a striking space with red velour jurors' chairs and blue carpet—and took her place at the massive oak plaintiff's table. Two minutes later, the court was in session.

"The defense calls Dr. Jacob Rosen."

Jake Rosen. Maybe he was why she felt edgy. She had met him last March, when she needed a second autopsy in the Jose Terrell shooting and had arranged to helicopter him to a New Jersey field next to the morgue—actually paid out of her own pocket!—so he could confirm the bullets that killed Terrell were fired by the cops while Terrell had his hands up in surrender.

Rosen had bounded out of the copter like a fashion-challenged Frankenstein with the unkempt hair of a mad scientist. The hair was long and thick, brown peppered with a few strands of gray; she'd had a ridiculous impulse to comb it for him just to feel it under her fingers. He carried a folded raincoat on top of a weatherbeaten black briefcase so full of papers he couldn't fasten the clasp, but he was superbly professional; his findings were so thorough the detective who fired the fatal shots struck a plea bargain, the city paid damages to the boy's mother, and the case never came to trial.

Now here was Rosen again, six months later, testifying for the defense. Manny knew that private experts could work for anyone they wanted, but she still felt betrayed. He'd been so patient with her, so cooperative. She felt he'd been as outraged as she was by the first, obviously bogus, coroner's report in the Terrell case. He seemed to care about truth then; now she knew his testimony could be sold to the highest bidder.

Manny barely looked up when he came in. She knew what he was going to say, but her own forensic expert had assured her that his opinion was a load of crap. So what if she'd briefly—momentarily—thought him attractive? He was Judas incarnate.

Today as he walked to the witness chair he looked like nothing more than some high-priced egghead from central casting trotted out by the cops to rationalize their bad behavior. Manny knew he was only forty-four, but under the courtroom lights he looked older. And he needed to go to a Pilates perfect-posture class to cure his slouching shoulders. He was wearing a black suit, a white shirt, and a skinny black tie. If he had spiky hair instead of the mad-scientist kind he'd have looked like an aging eighties British punk rocker. In the months since she'd seen him he'd grown a mustache. Facial hair from the seventies, clothes from the eighties—What was his problem? Hadn't anyone told him he was living in the twenty-first century?

Under direct examination, Rosen testified that he thought the police could easily be blameless, citing a berry aneurysm of the brain. *Blameless!* "So to sum up," the lawyer said, "in your professional opinion, you feel that Miss Carramia's death was *not* due to any action on the part of the police officers in question."

"That's correct," Rosen said, turning to the jury. "In my opinion, there is a reasonable degree of medical certainty that the decedent died of natural causes."

Yeah. Like the sidewalk stood up and cracked her skull open.

"Thank you for your honesty, doctor." The defense attorney favored the jury with one of his nauseatingly smarmy smiles. "No further questions."

Manny rose from behind the plaintiff's table and approached the witness. She was going to eat him up and spit him out.

"Dr. Rosen, how much are you being paid for your testimony today?"

"My fee is five thousand dollars—for my time, not my testimony."

Manny raised a scornful eyebrow. "A *day*?"

"Yes."

He hadn't charged *her* that much last March to do a second autopsy. Maybe if she'd outbid the defense she could have recruited him for Essie's parents.

"I see," she said. "You work for the City of New York, correct?"

"I'm deputy chief medical examiner. But I'm testifying in this case in my private capacity as a physician and a forensic pathologist."

Blood was in the water and she was the shark. "In your role for the city, isn't it important to have a good relationship with the police?"

He crossed his legs, unfazed. Manny noticed that his suit jacket had been patched. *What? Couldn't afford a new suit at five thousand per? What a loser.*

"Of course," he said, "but that doesn't affect my opinion."

"Doctor, are you acquainted with Dr. Justin West, medical examiner for the State of New Jersey, and Dr. Sanjay Sumet, the forensic pathologist who testified for the plaintiff in this case?"

"Indeed. They're both fine men and fine doctors."

"Doctors West and Sumet agree that Miss Carramia died as the result of a blow to the head. But you claim she died of natural causes—a brain aneurysm. Is that right?"

"Yes. As I've just testified, a ruptured berry aneurysm." Rosen shifted back in his chair, which creaked under his weight. The witness box wasn't designed to accommodate such long legs. Manny hoped he was as uncomfortable in his lies as he was in his body. But there was no strain detectable in his voice. "My opinion is based on the material I've reviewed: the autopsy report, witness statements, and my dissection of the brain, which had been retained by the medical examiner."

"But there's nothing in her medical records to indicate she had such a condition."

Rosen turned to the judge. "Is that a question?"

Smug prig.

"I'll rephrase," Manny said quickly. "Was there anything in her medical history to suggest she suffered from this"—she cast a meaningful look at the jury—"rare condition?"

Rosen shrugged. "There probably wouldn't be."

She shook her head as if she'd never heard anything so outlandish. "Then isn't your opinion awfully convenient for the police? In fact, aren't you handing them a gift-wrapped Get Out of Jail Free card?"

All six lawyers for the defense leaped to their feet, like cheerleaders at the big game. "Objection!" one shouted.

Manny rolled her eyes at them. "It's a figure of speech."

"She's being argumentative," said another.

The judge grinned. "What else is new?" Manny started to speak but he waved her off. "Overruled," he said.

"Thank you, your honor." She turned back to Rosen. "Doctor, isn't it true that, in cases such as this, the testimony of the officers involved is often unreliable?"

He leaned forward. "Not necessarily."

Got him! "Really?" She brandished a document. "This is an abstract of a paper given at a meeting of the American Academy of Forensic Sciences in February 1993, based on a study of twenty-one police takedown death cases. It concludes that pathologists should *not* rely on police testimony in such cases because it's often inaccurate, possibly due to stress or simple dishonesty. Are you familiar with the paper?"

"I believe so." Was he winking at her?

"Didn't you write it, Dr. Rosen?"

How can he be so unruffled? I've nailed him.

"You're missing the point," he said. "In those cases, the police testimony conflicted with the science. Here, it doesn't."

Manny turned on him, hair flying out of her hastily engineered chignon. "Do you expect this jury to believe that she just *happened* to die while being arrested? What does your science say about implausible coincidence?"

Rosen tapped his fingertips on the wooden railing, the first sign of anger. "It's not a coincidence," he said, keeping his voice under control. "The bursting of a natural aneurysm can be brought on by emotional stress or physical exertion, like getting caught shoplifting and struggling with the police."

Uh-oh. Juries didn't like it when you called an expert witness a big fat jerk, which she was tempted to do. But this last from him was a point for the defense.

"Dr. Rosen," she said, recovering, "two of your colleagues have testified that Miss Carramia suffered a subdural hemorrhage, which is nearly always indicative of blunt force trauma. Are they lying?"

Rosen rubbed his temple. *If I'm lucky, maybe he's having an aneurysm of his own.*

"Not at all. Without fully dissecting the brain, it was an easy mistake." He addressed the jury in a gentle voice, as though he were Mister Rogers and they lived in his neighborhood. "An aneurysm is like a very small balloon. When this one burst, the blood flowed through the very thin arachnoid layer, which is the inner membrane covering the brain, to the outer thicker dura covering, creating a subdural hemorrhage from natural causes. It's true that most subdural hemorrhages are due to trauma. This one wasn't." To demonstrate, Rosen formed a ball with his cupped hands and then opened the top one as though they were hinged at the pinkies.

Lord, Manny thought. He's becoming taller in the witness stand. More authoritative. And the jury's starting to believe him!

"Additionally," Rosen continued, "when the top of the skull was removed at autopsy, blood leaking from the postmortem incisions pooled inside the lower part of the skull, making it look like an even bigger subdural bleed. It could easily be mistaken for a traumatic injury, but it's actually consistent with the officers' testimony that the victim's head never struck the ground."

"In your opinion," Manny snarled, watching uncertainty cloud the jurors' faces. *If that pontificating hired gun persuades them—*

"An opinion," Rosen said, "which is backed by the vomitus the medical examiner found on the victim's clothing. Vomiting is a classic sign of a leaking berry aneurysm."

Manny felt her blood pressure spike. Her hair fell wetly across her cheeks. The son of a bitch was twisting the girl's suffering to get the cops off the hook. "That vomit," she said, "is evidence of the trauma six policemen inflicted on a one-hundred-and-five-pound girl. Or didn't you read Dr. Sumet's report?"

"I did. But what he failed to note was that the vomitus recovered from her jacket sleeve contained eggs, tomatoes, and tortillas."

"Exactly. Which the victim ate for breakfast."

"Counselor," Rosen said, condescension dripping from the word, "according to her family, Miss Carramia ate at ten-thirty a.m. If she'd vomited as a result of the arrest four hours later, the food would have been mostly digested. It was not. This is proof that vomiting *preceded* the arrest. The girl died of natural causes. That's what the science tells us."

Manny shot a glance at the jury. *They believe him.* She felt sick, cold. *Counterattack. But how?* "Dr. Rosen," she said, "apart from all this suspect speculation, you don't have any solid evidence about what happened to Miss Carramia, do you?"

He leaned back, looking maddeningly comfortable. She envisioned him with pipe and slippers. "The body always tells the story," he said. "Not only about how people died but how they lived."

She felt a shiver of fear. *Never mind that he's an arrogant jerk. Just finish your cross.*

"Come on, Doctor. Now you're telling us you can read a body like some psychic with tea leaves?" *Mistake! Never ask a question you can't answer. What the hell am I doing?* "Go ahead. Enlighten us. What could you know about the death of Esmeralda Carramia that hasn't been covered by two years' worth of investigation?"

"For one thing," he said, "she was a gang member."

Manny heard a gasp and looked behind her. Mrs. Carramia sat with her face covered by her hands, sobbing.

"The evidence is in the autopsy photos," Rosen went on. "Miss Carramia had a pachuco tattoo."

Manny breathed a sigh of relief. "You mean the crucifix? A religious symbol?"

Now Rosen stared directly at the jurors. "A simple homemade cross with three small dashes on top. It's a gang sign, often made with ink or ashes. Hers also had a fourth mark on the lower right side." His voice lowered. The jury leaned forward to listen. "This indicates heroin addiction. In the really rough gangs it's a badge of honor. It's usually a prison tattoo, by the way."

Manny felt dizzy. She saw Mr. Carramia, his face ashen, lead his wife from the room. They looked like a pair of children caught with their hands in a candy box. Rosen had transformed their angelic little girl into a shoplifting drug-addicted gangbanger. And her parents had known it all along. "Move to strike," she said tonelessly. *Lost. I've lost.*

A defense lawyer was on his feet. "Counsel opened the door when she had Miss Carramia's mother testify about her child's spotless record."

The judge nodded. "She sure did."

The others in the room, Essie's friends and the friends of the cops, sat silently for a moment and then began to talk, heedless of the judge's gavel. Only Rosen was still, sitting in the witness box like a king on his throne or, Manny thought, like my executioner.

"No further questions," she whispered.

CHAPTER ONE

It was Jake's idea of a perfect rainy Friday night. The trial was over, the truth had prevailed—too bad about Manny Manfreda; she had done a good job but she didn't have the right evidence—and now he was alone in his Upper East Side brownstone kitchen, eating Chinese food, reading a treatise on blood spatter, and listening to Duke Ellington's soundtrack of *Anatomy of a Murder*. Brilliant movie, inspiring music. *Peace, it's wonderful.*

Alongside his take-out containers, piles of paperwork cluttered the top of his chrome-and-red Formica table; he'd tackle it over the weekend. His kitchen held a motley group of appliances: a recently purchased commercial stainless steel refrigerator, an avocado-green stove from the sixties, a white porcelain double sink from the fifties. The countertops were fifties Formica in green geometrical patterns; the metal cabinets, painted and repainted over the years, were a drab beige. A butcher-block island, scarred by years of white rings from wet plates and glasses, stood in faded glory in the center of the space. French doors in the back opened into a garden, converted by neglect into living quarters for a few happy squirrels, some pigeons, and an occasional chair.

Jake had bought the five-story brownstone in the mid-1980s,

shortly after being hired at the ME's office. He could only afford it because it was north of Ninety-sixth Street near Harlem, in those days not the nicest of neighborhoods. But he didn't see it as an investment or even a possession. He saw New York's history: the wealthy who had once populated the area, the careful work of nineteenth-century stonemasons, and the varied texture of the constantly changing community. When he finally had the money to do some work on the place, it was so full of forensic teaching materials and artifacts, he had no idea where to start. Besides, he didn't have the time. This was New York. People died by the hundreds every day. He *never* had the time.

The music stopped, and he stopped eating and stared at his food. The sauce on his sesame chicken, he realized, was nearly the consistency of human blood. He picked up a knife, dipped it, and spattered the sauce across the kitchen table and the wall behind it, as though someone had stabbed the chicken from behind.

The phone rang. Damn. He picked it up. "Rosen."

"Miss me?"

The two words gave him a jolt of pleasure. The only voice allowed to intrude into his solitude was Pete Harrigan's—any time and any place. Pete, thirty years Jake's senior, was one of only two people on this earth Jake loved. The other was his brother, Sam, and Sam didn't have intrusion privileges.

"Sure I miss you." Jake studied the mess on the table. "In fact, I was just thinking about you. The influence of knife length on cast-off blood spatter patterns."

"I'm flattered," Harrigan said. "But you should be out on a date. Weren't you seeing that fingerprint expert from—"

"Broke it off," Jake said quickly, feeling a flash of pain. "Too soon after my divorce."

"Trouble with women, trouble in the office. I hear you've had a go-round with Chief Pederson. Too much private work, not enough time serving the city." Harrigan had once been chief himself. Retired now, he obviously still had tentacles inside the ME's office. "How is my old friend Charles Pederson? Does he still resent me now that he's replaced me as chief medical examiner?"

"Still the same where you're concerned," Jake said. "Hey, you're the one who taught me any medical examiner worth a damn pisses off the powers that be. Comes with the territory."

"And you were my best student. Developed *pissing off* into a specialty. How's Wally?" Harrigan was given to abrupt changes of subject.

"Blossoming. The man's a godsend. I thank you for him every day."

Dr. Walter Winnick—Wally—was a protégé whom Harrigan had recommended to Jake. The man had a clubfoot, but his mind sprinted to invariably accurate conclusions; Jake couldn't have handled his workload without him.

"Glad to hear it."

"How's Elizabeth?" Jake asked.

"Fine. The woman's going to be New Jersey's next governor. Ever since she married that Markis fellow, though, she's pretty much stopped visiting. If I want to see my daughter, I have to go to New Jersey, and even then I have to make an appointment through her press agent."

There was a pause. Unusual, Jake thought. Pete was generally so voluble Jake couldn't shut him up. He could hear Harrigan's labored breathing. Sick, Jake wondered, or in trouble? "What's up?"

"Let's talk shop."

"Sure," Jake said, relieved. "You heard about the Carramia case?"

"As a matter of fact, no. For once I'm not calling about your cases, I'm calling about one of mine."

"Shoot," Jake said.

A hesitation, a cough. "I was wondering if you'd like to come up here and help me decipher some bones."

Since his retirement, Dr. Peter Harrigan lived in the hamlet of Turner, a little town on a big lake two hours north of the city. Jake got there at six the next morning. He met Harrigan at his home, a white Cape Cod cottage with yellow shutters, which looked from the outside more like a doll's house than the residence of a globally respected forensic pathologist.

The two men embraced. "We'll have to take your car even though I hate seeing the street through your floorboards," Pete said. "My Suburban's sick." He piled a box of autopsy tools, a camera, and a few body bags into the backseat of Jake's old, falling apart Oldsmobile and brought two mugs of coffee to the front. He was wearing the same blue Polartec jacket Jake had given him seven years ago on the eve of Pete's departure; Jake had on the dark green oilskin Marianna had bought him on their only trip to London.

"You do realize," Jake said, as Pete backed the Camaro out of the driveway, "that you live in the geographical center of nowhere."

Harrigan grinned. "It's exciting, though. Big-time crime. Just last week our mayor shot an elk out of season. Town's still debating how much to fine him."

Jake swallowed hot coffee. It was bitter and strong; considering his sleep deprivation he was going to need a lot of it. "You lived in New York for over thirty years."

"I got over it."

After almost four decades in forensic pathology, Harrigan had retired to the country to please his wife, Dolores, who died less than three years later. Bored with fishing, he had taken on the post of Baxter County medical examiner, which meant signing off on one or two death certificates a week and doing two or three autopsies a month. At seventy-two, he was the oldest sitting medical examiner in the state of New York.

"So explain," Jake said. "Why did I drive up here in the middle of the night?"

"To get here before the excavation starts up again."

"Excavation of what?"

"That field in the distance."

"And they're digging on a Saturday morning?"

"Apparently," Pete said, "the building of a shopping mall waits for no man—or bones."

They were traveling on a two-lane road, passing trees, not houses. "A shopping mall? Up here?"

"Rumor has it the governor's going to give the Senecas rights to build a casino. The town fathers are half mad with the prospect of all those tourists, so naturally they want to give them a place to spend their winnings. And what more appropriate location than in back of the Turner insane asylum?"

Jake grunted. "Fat chance anyone will win."

Pete glanced at him, amused. "You never were much of a gambler, were you."

"Only at love. And look what that won me: a monthly alimony check."

Jake still felt the divorce of his parents with almost the same pain he'd experienced with his own. He remembered hugging his father's leg the last time he walked out the door. His younger brother, Sam, had been a baby, couldn't even stand yet, and didn't know what was going on. But Jake's childhood had gone downhill from that moment. After twenty years of being a medical examiner, he was convinced that the biggest risk factors for murder were love and marriage. He believed the marriage vow should say, I promise to love, honor, and not kill you. He had chosen a career as an ME both to improve society and to prove that a delinquent kid could make something of his life. The time it took to make a marriage work wasn't compatible with his goals.

They continued down the road, sunlight just starting to peek through the trees. "They'd just broken ground on their god-forsaken center early yesterday morning," Pete said, "when the backhoe brought up the upper part of a skull. The lower jaw, the mandible, was missing, probably carried off with the dirt before the crew realized what they had. In a construction site like this, the first instinct is to ignore anything that gets in the way, but the backhoe driver called the authorities and they called me. I found an ulna and a tibia to go along with the skull and ordered a shut-down." Harrigan shot Jake a look. "I leave you to guess what the developer said the delay would cost him."

Jake smiled into his mug. "An arm and a leg?"

"Just so."

"I'm guessing those aren't an old settler's bones or you wouldn't have brought me up here."

"You got it. Within an hour, the scene was crawling with people: the developer himself—R. Seward Reynolds—his lackeys, his lawyers, the mayor, the sheriff, half the town council, and the ever-lovely Marge Crespy, doyenne of the Turner Historical Society."

"Good God!"

"All of them seemed eager for the remains to be a settler. I told them, *Impossible*. I needed to take care of something else I couldn't put off yesterday afternoon. I called you last night for help on this issue."

Jake got the familiar queasy feeling in his stomach that came with the suspicion of corruption. "Sure. A settler means no fights over Indian burial grounds, no worries about a crime scene. They can just rebury the bones somewhere else and get on with the mall." He looked at his friend and mentor, feeling the anger in Pete's bearing. "Do *you* think it's a Native American?"

"I found an incisor. It isn't shovel-shaped. The skull has rectangular eye sockets and a triangular nasal opening. You tell me."

"Caucasian."

Harrigan nodded. "And a good thing, too, as far as the mayor's concerned. He was apoplectic at the prospect of a dispute over native land."

"Then what's the problem?"

"The bones were normal weight and nonporous."

"Meaning they're probably less than fifty years old."

"And they weren't sticky. The tongue doesn't lie."

Jake imagined Miss Crespy's reaction when Pete touched his tongue to the remains, looking for stickiness caused by porous texture and a lack of organic material. "The death was recent. You told them that?"

"Of course. But with all that lovely tax revenue at stake, they're hardly inclined to take the word of a bone-licker."

"That's why you called me in? To back you up?"

"Partly. And there are practical considerations. My hands and eyes are no longer as sharp as my mind. My heart isn't getting any stronger. I'd already decided to step down as ME at the end of the year." He paused. "This may be the last interesting case I ever get. It would be fitting if we did it together."

He's pleading with me, Jake thought, struck by a tone he had never heard before. Why? It was easy to remember Harrigan as the vigorous pathologist who had mentored him from the moment they'd met at the morgue at Bellevue Hospital; Jake had still been in medical school and the ME office had used the old Bellevue morgue. Now he studied his friend like the scientist Pete had trained him to be.

What he saw was a man whose hands shook with faint tremors, whose skin had become papery and translucent, whose watery eyes had lost some of their clarity and focus. *He's old. Older and more tired than I've ever seen him before.*

"Of course I'll help," Jake said, feeling deeply moved. "I'm honored."

Pete snorted. "Jesus, don't go soft on me. Have some dignity, man."

"Be polite," Jake warned, "or you're not getting your Johnnie Walker Blue."

Pete's eyes widened. *"Blue?"*

"Right there in my overnight bag. A little present from your most ardent admirer."

"We're here," Pete said, stopping the car. "Let's get this over with quickly so we can go back home and drink it."

There were already more than a dozen cars parked on the scraggly grass at the edge of the construction site, including the sheriff's cruiser. Beyond stretched land that had once been forest. Dozens of trees had already been felled, the logs waiting in neat pyramids to be hauled off to the sawmill. Pete and Jake set off toward the backhoe, a mute monster standing at the side of the field, impotent as a child's toy. Fifteen people were clustered nearby, all men but for one woman, fiftyish and fierce beneath her blue peacoat—indubitably, Jake thought, Miss Crespy. Most of the men were wearing jeans, flannel shirts, and work boots, the universal garb of construction workers. Three more were standing a few yards from the rest, two wearing khakis and open-collared shirts, the other a beer belly and a badge. As soon as she saw Harrigan, the woman joined them.

"The one on the left's the mayor," Pete whispered. "Next to him's the Reynolds foreman. The other's the sheriff, obviously."

The group had clearly been waiting for Harrigan to arrive. They looked at Rosen with the suspicion reserved for strangers in a small town.

"This here's Dr. Jacob Rosen from the New York City medical examiner's office," Pete said. "Mayor Bob Stevenson, Sheriff Joe

Fisk, Harry King—he's in charge of construction—and, of course, Miss Crespy."

All of them shook hands with Jake except Fisk, who turned his back, muttering something Jake couldn't make out.

"Dr. Rosen is the best there is," Pete said—too cheerfully, Jake thought. "I've asked him to help with the disinterment."

Mayor Stevenson looked less than thrilled. "Come on, Pete," he said. "You know the town can't afford some fancy New York—"

"Dr. Rosen is volunteering his time as a personal favor to me. So let's not waste our opportunity."

The group arrived at the edge of the gash the giant machine had made in the ground the previous afternoon. A black tarp had been laid out nearby, bearing two bones and the upper part of a skull. None of the spectators seemed eager to get too close.

Jake crouched next to the tarp and picked up the skull. It was as Pete described: normal weight, nonporous. Clearly less than fifty years old.

Miss Crespy stepped forward. She was wearing a turtleneck sweater under her coat, neat blue jeans, and a pair of L.L. Bean rubber boots, reminding Jake of his first-grade teacher, a woman he had loathed. "It could have been in the ground for ages," she said peremptorily. "Who can tell?"

"I can," Jake said, "and so can Dr. Harrigan."

"We didn't find any iron nails or decayed coffin wood like you usually find near a settler's bones," Pete explained patiently, his voice hoarse. "Besides, these bones are relatively new."

"I say we let Mr. King get back to work," the sheriff said, standing over Jake like an overseer with a slave.

Jake looked up into an expression of pure malice. "Not until we examine the bones," he said. "Right now they represent a puzzle we have to solve."

"Can you say for sure the bones are new?"

"Not yet. That's why Dr. Harrigan—" He stopped mid-sentence and pointed to the excavated ground, where a wide swath of topsoil had been removed, revealing the dirt beneath. Most of it was dark brown and compact. But to the left of where the bones had been found, patches of earth were lighter, less firmly packed. "Pete," he said, "take a look at this."

Harrigan bent, Jake noted, with some difficulty. "My God," he breathed.

"What's this?" Sheriff Fisk asked, exasperated. "What are we playing, Twenty Questions? You're delaying the most important project ever to come Turner's way because you found some bones a dog probably dragged here. It's inexcusable."

Jake stood, making it a point to ignore him. "When you bury a body, it disturbs the ground. Even after you fill it back in, the earth's never the same. Even if the grass has grown back, underneath the topsoil it's still obvious." He indicated the border between the two shades of earth. "You can see here where the ground has been dug up and replaced."

"So who gives a damn?" the sheriff snarled.

Jake stared at him coldly. "You will. Judging by the number of disturbed areas, there's more than one body down there."

CHAPTER TWO

ONE BY ONE, the bones were painstakingly brought from the ground and laid on the tarp. Jake examined each of them, heedless of the increasingly hot sun, his mind electric with excitement. It's like playing with God's jigsaw puzzle, he thought, placing the bones together in their anatomical positions. Soon he was working by himself. Pete, weakened by the heat, had gone back to Jake's car for a rest; the others, quickly bored, decided to drive into town for breakfast. The construction workers had been sent home for the day. The foreman stayed and watched from the construction trailer.

Jake was relieved. The human body was to him magnificent, and its building blocks, its bones, never ceased to enthrall him. There was more beauty in the creation of man than there was in sublime music. He sometimes felt, as he felt now, that the mute bones were eloquent, if only he could fully understand their language. He formed skeletons—three men and, yes, a woman. What stories could they tell? he wondered. Who had brought them to this field and buried them?

When he was finished, he went back to the car to get Pete. "You won't believe it," he told his friend. He knew it was up to them to restore some measure of what the skeletons had lost; it was a debt the living owed the dead. Since these people could no longer speak for themselves, it was their duty to speak for them.

They walked back to the field together and stared down at the skeletons. Pete had been silent since Jake awakened him; now he seemed in a distant place, transfixed by the evidence of so much death.

"Look," Jake said, "the last bone I found was the mandible belonging to the woman. It matches the upper part of the skull the backhoe dug up originally."

Pete stared, shuddered. The movement seemed to rouse him from his trance. "You're right," he said, as he stooped to examine it with the upper part of its skull. "We'd best get the bones to the morgue. Baxter Community Hospital's five miles away. I'll call the others from the trailer and tell them to meet us there." Pete checked his pockets. "Left their numbers in your car. Be back in a bit."

He's sick, Jake realized. It would indeed be their last case together. He was sure of it.

By four that afternoon, the entire group had reassembled in a basement room next to the morgue. The four skeletons were laid out on four stretchers inside the morgue—not complete, Jake knew, but able to tell a partial story. One woman, three men. But there was so much more to be learned from the bones: height, age, race, cause of death, potentially identifying old fractures, and when they had died.

In life they had had names, faces, jobs, opinions, emotions. Now they were reduced to a series of numbers written on pieces of paper at the foot of each stretcher. The audience stood solemnly; even Sheriff Fisk seemed awed.

"How do you know Four's a woman?" Miss Crespy asked.

Jake indicated the top edge of the socket where the left eye had been. "That's called the glabella—the brow ridge. In a woman it's smooth. In men, bumpy." He saw that some in the audience were feeling their own eyebrows and stifled a grin. Happened every time. "Same with the external occipital protuberance on the back of the skull." He turned the skull around and ran a finger along its gently curved rear surface. "It's more prominent in males, smoother in females." He took a closer look at the upper jaw. "And she was young. Third molars haven't erupted."

Harrington set about taking measurements and dictating notes into a tape recorder. Jake could tell by the expression on his face that he was deeply emotional. "Skeleton Four, most bones present, female. In addition to the unerupted third molars, the lack of fusing of both clavicles medially indicates her age to be under twenty-two. Some clumps of dark hair up to six inches long adjacent to the vertex of the skull. All long bones of the upper and lower extremities are present. Right ribs eight and nine posteriorly show fractures. The amount of healing suggests these injuries were sustained approximately two weeks before death. The pitting pattern of the pubic symphysis indicates vaginal childbirth." Pete paused, taking in great gulps of air. "Sheriff, this young woman may have a child out there." His pallor seemed unearthly.

"Maybe you should get some air," Jake said.

Harrigan shook his head. "Let's finish. That scotch is beginning to sound awful good." He put the recorder to his mouth. "Skeleton Three. Here, too, most bones are present. Calcification of cartilage of first and second ribs, osteophytes in the thoracic and lumbar spine, and fused skull sutures mean he was at least thirty-five."

Jake turned to the group. "Those osteophytes are bony protuberances on the spinal column. They happen as you get older."

Harrington picked up the skull. "Here again some dark hair is present; this time it measures two inches in length. Notice the oval-shaped hole at the vertex through the parietal bones at the top of the skull. Looks to be about four by three inches. It's not post-mortem deterioration."

"You mean somebody bashed his head in?" Fisk asked.

"Not precisely. If it were a fresh fracture, the edges would be rough. I'd say he lived long enough for healing to occur, between two and six months, I'd estimate." He proffered the skull. "Care to feel it? Smooth."

Fisk recoiled. "No, thanks."

Jake had learned a long time ago that machismo was no indication of whether a person would lose his cool in an autopsy room. He knew burly police detectives who couldn't watch him wield a scalpel and petite female MEs who could finish two autopsies and go out and eat sushi.

"That looks like a surgical procedure," Jake said. "There probably was a replacement with a metal plate but, if so, we didn't find it."

"Maybe it's still in the ground," Harrigan said. "Somebody's going to have to go back and look."

Fisk made a note. "Why would a doctor cut a piece out of someone's head?"

"War wound," Jake said. "It'll help if you can find the plate."

Harrington turned the skull around so it faced them. "Notice the dental fillings. Proof positive that these aren't settlers. The probable cause of death is this displaced fracture of the second cervical vertebra—the axis—which would have damaged the spinal cord."

Amazing, Jake thought. *He saw more than I did. Always pay attention to the body. It's telling you its secrets.* "Broken neck," he translated for the group.

Harrigan pointed to a dirty band of elastic that encircled the skeleton's pelvic bones.

"Is that . . . what's left of his clothes?" Miss Crespy asked.

"Looks like it." Harrigan gently removed the elastic remnant and handed it to Jake, who had put on new surgical gloves. Jake placed it on a clean paper catch cloth to avoid the loss of any trace evidence.

"Came from a pair of men's briefs," Jake noted. "There's some writing on it." He took the elastic to the sink and slowly washed off the dirt into a plastic container. "Could be a laundry mark." He leaned over it with a magnifying glass. "Can't quite make it out. Anybody have a flashlight?"

Fisk handed him his Maglite.

"It's hard to read, but I think it's . . . T.M.H. 631217. Do you recognize the initials, Pete?"

There was no answer. Pete was bent over, arms around his stomach; his breathing was ragged, his face white. A word flashed unbidden into Jake's mind: *cancer.*

Pete straightened. "His own initials?" he answered. "Maybe he had monogrammed underpants, like they do for kids at camp."

"Maybe," Jake said. "It's something to go on." All he wanted was to get Pete home and in bed, find out if his diagnosis was right, and see what he could do about it. But Pete pressed on.

"Skeleton Two is less complete than Four or Three. Skull sutures aren't fused and there's a lack of rib calcification. Puts him close to thirty." He picked up the skull. "Eye sockets look Caucasian. The pelvis confirms it's male. Left humerus present. A little clump of hair is still attached to a small amount of grave wax formed from the fat on the front of the pubic bone."

He moved on. "Skeleton One. Defleshed bones of left arm and hand. Not much to work with." He eyed the group.

Sheriff Fisk's face was red. It was obvious he was finding the facts uncomfortable. *Funny. You'd think he'd be fascinated. For him, it's the case of a lifetime.* But all Fisk asked was, "What's this going to mean for the mall?"

"It means," Jake said, "your construction site's a crime scene."

Back at the cottage at last, Jake made them a dinner of bacon and eggs. They had eaten the same meal countless late nights in the lab, whipped up on a hot plate in their office's tiny kitchen, and he was feeling nostalgic.

Nostalgic and worried. Color had returned to Pete's face, and there'd been no recurrence of stomach cramps, but still it was obvious his friend was failing. *His eyes are jaundiced. Must be drinking or sick. How do I bring up the subject? He's one proud son of a bitch.*

After dinner, they went to Pete's study and opened the bottle of Johnnie Walker Blue, the granddaddy of blended scotches and, Jake knew, Harrigan's favorite guilty pleasure—that and a foul-smelling pipe. Jake had received the bottle as a gift from the National Organization of Law Enforcement Officers after he'd delivered a lecture on the relationship between police, medicine, and the crime scene. He'd been tempted to sample it but had saved it to share with Harrigan; now he wasn't so sure it was the right thing to do.

Pete sipped, puffed on his pipe, breathed contentment. "We had some interesting cases together, didn't we? Remember the 'ghost spots' murder? The Adam Gardiner case?"

"Use that one to teach about blood spatter," Jake agreed. "It was one of the first autopsies I watched you perform."

Gardiner had been found dead in his garage, naked, facedown in his own blood, a gash over his right eye. His body had more than a hundred red and brown bruises, some small, some large. There was blood in the house as well, smears and drops over the kitchen floor. The police thought it was murder. They shipped the body to Harrigan at the morgue.

"But the gash on the head couldn't bleed that much," Harrigan went on. "And the drops on the floor were evenly spaced. When I saw the blood spatter I knew. Gardiner had been walking slowly; there was no killer coming up behind him. The autopsy findings confirmed it. He had undiagnosed untreated tuberculosis that bled into his lungs; he couldn't breathe and was coughing blood. He was too drunk to call nine-one-one. The bruises were in different stages of healing, indicative of an alcoholic who keeps hitting edges of chairs and walls. *Fall-down drunk*, as the saying goes. It's how he got that gash over his eye: he fell. His death was natural. He killed himself—by drinking."

This was the kind of talk Jake adored. He had some of it with Wally, but his assistant would need more experience to know its full pleasure. "They never taught us in med school that when a person coughs up blood, it mixes with air and forms bubbles," he said. "But you did. So the drops dry with clear centers, unlike blood drops from a cut. The bubble pops when it hits the ground. After it dries, the center appears pale as a ghost. Ghost spots."

Pete raised his glass in triumph. "Good work, that. The emphasis today on DNA takes away from the importance of paying attention to small details at the scene and the autopsy. It's made us lazy."

Jake joined him in his salute. "You made me realize a good ME is a scientific detective. The obvious answers aren't always right, and the right answers aren't always obvious." He took a deep breath. "Pete, are you all right?"

The older man looked at him sharply. "What do you mean?"

"Today, for example. You couldn't take the sun; you doubled over in the morgue; you were pale as paper. I don't like it."

Pete poured himself another drink, swallowed it in a gulp, and poured again, leaving this one on the desk. "I'm fine. Really."

"I don't believe you. I'll get off this, I promise, but if you're sick, tell me."

Sadness and pain crept into Harrigan's eyes. "Jake, I—"

"Go on."

"I miss her, is all. I miss my wife Dolores."

That's not all, Jake thought. Not by a long shot. But if his friend didn't want to talk, there was no way to force him. Pete had always been secretive, sometimes revealing what he wanted Jake to know only by leading him to that knowledge indirectly. *I'll find out the rest when he's ready and not until then. Be patient.*

By Sunday night, Jake was back home reviewing autopsy photos and witness statements in preparation for testimony he had to give in a murder trial the next morning. If it hadn't been for the court appearance, he'd have stayed in Turner and taken his first vacation day in God knows how long to keep working with Harrigan.

But the truth was they'd done just about all they could do for the time being. They'd photographed the skeletons, concentrating on the broken vertebra, cracked ribs, and skull defect. They'd collected samples of the soil where the stomachs would have been in hopes of discovering what the decedents had eaten—a wild chance, they knew, but Harrigan would send it to the lab all the same, along with the hair for toxicology. When Jake finally drove off around seven, Harrigan was still at the hospital, x-raying the bones.

Jake didn't hear from Harrigan again until Tuesday afternoon. It was already past three, and Jake still had two more autopsies ahead of him. He was sorting through messages in his office, putting aside everything that wasn't marked *Urgent*, when the phone rang.

"Have a minute?"

"Maybe two, but that's all. What's up?"

"There's been a breakthrough, but it's a good-news/bad-news situation." There was tension in Pete's voice, but at least it was strong.

"Go on."

"The good news is we know where the bodies came from. The bad news is everyone's so happy with the answer, they're about to restart work on the mall."

"Slow down. How'd you find out about the bodies?"

"I didn't. Marge Crespy did. Remember the initials on the elastic?"

"Of course."

"Turns out they stand for Turner Mental Hospital. As long as I've lived here, it's been called the Turner Psychiatric Institute, but Marge is the historian and knew the earlier names—it began as a home for the feebleminded. Anyway, I got in touch with Hank Ewing—Henry Ewing, Nobel laureate, dean of the Catskill Medical School, once head of Turner, friend of mine—and he filled me in on the place's history. I'll tell you when we see each other. The point is, they treated nearly ten thousand people over the decades, among them hundreds of indigents."

"And Ewing says that when they died they were buried in the *field*?" Jake asked.

"It's not far from the hospital—which is closed down, by the way. I guess they ran out of crazies in Baxter County, or it got too expensive to keep them. Marge found no record of its being a potter's field, and as far as Sheriff Fisk and Mayor Stevenson are concerned, the case is closed. Indigents. Untraceable. The backhoe rides again at dawn."

The queasy feeling returned to Jake's stomach. *Corruption.* "They're going too fast," he said. "They should at least wait until you have the tox and DNA results."

"Right. And I need to reshoot the X-rays on the Skeleton Two humerus. Something went wrong with the film."

"But Fisk and Stevenson don't want to hold up construction."

Harrigan sighed. "You know, I'd just as soon let 'em go on. I have to live in this town, and I'm not a big fan of crucifixion."

Jake felt a surge of anger. "Quitting?"

"Not really." He sounded suddenly very tired. "I went over to the site again Monday, looking for the plate from the skull of Skeleton Three. God knows, Fisk wasn't going to do it. Anyway, I found it. Fits perfectly. You can take a look tomorrow."

"Pete, there's no way I can get there. I've got a month's work here to be finished by Friday."

"But who else is going to help me identify the other three bodies?"

Sly fox. The other three? "You've ID'd one of them?"

"From the laundry mark." Harrigan sounded smug.

"Assuming the man was wearing his own underpants."

"According to a logbook at the historical society, patient number 631217 was one James Albert Lyons. Height, race, and age match the skeletal findings. I'm trying to locate his next of kin."

"You don't waste any time."

"At my age, time's precious. So haul your ass up here and help out."

"Really, I can't. Pederson will have my head if I take time off, and I'm being deposed on a double murder on Thursday."

"Jake, it's urgent!"

Despite himself, he was getting annoyed. "Why? It's routine work. Get one of the hospital staffers to help."

"It's not the identification. I have to talk to you."

"What about?"

Pete's voice dropped to a whisper. "It has to be in person. *Has* to be."

He's going to tell me about the cancer. "I'll come up Friday night, then. It's the soonest I can make it."

A pause.

"Okay?"

Pete sighed. *The sound of despair.* "I can live with it."

CHAPTER THREE

JAKE KNOCKED on the door: no answer. He tried the knob: locked. "Pete, you home?"

Silence.

Jake walked to the back of the house. The kitchen lights were on, the door open. Jake entered. There was a dirty frying pan in the sink, along with a single plate and some cutlery. Pete had made himself a steak for dinner.

"Pete?"

He moved through to the living room. One light was on, but there was no sign of his friend. Frightened now, Jake opened the door to the master bedroom, hoping Pete had simply gone to sleep after his meal. The bedclothes were rumpled, but there was no one on the bed. Jake could feel his heart pounding; the quiet was oppressive.

Only the study, where just a week ago they had talked of ghost spots and shared the finest scotch in the world, was unexplored.

"You in there?" He opened the door.

Pete was slumped at his desk, a book open in his hands. In two steps Jake was at his friend's side, taking his pulse, feeling for life but finding none.

He let out a little moan. *I should have talked Pederson into letting me go. I should have spent more time with him. Told him I loved him like a father. Too late. Dear God, forgive me. Too late.*

Verify. He bent over the body and tried to move the jaw, confirming the presence of rigor mortis. Then he gently lifted Harrigan's face from the desktop. Lividity had developed, but it wasn't fixed yet. Jake pressed his thumb against Pete's right cheek, noting that an oval of pale skin appeared and then faded away. Time of death, Jake knew, was about three-thirty, four hours before he walked through the door.

Science finished, he sat in the chair facing the desk and let himself weep.

A small private funeral mass was held for Dr. Peter Harrigan in the local parish of his Catholic church in the Queens neighborhood where he and Dolores spent most of their married life. Given Elizabeth's position as New Jersey's U.S. Attorney, there would be a large reception afterward at her home, but Pete had wanted a simple ceremony, and Elizabeth had honored his wishes. Jake spotted her in the front row, her head buried against the shoulder of a man—Daniel Markis, Jake figured. He had never met her husband, but who else could it be? There were two girls on one side of her, a boy on Markis's right. Their children, but Jake couldn't remember their names. The sight of them was disconcerting. It had been fifteen years since he'd last seen her, and though Pete had told him of her marriage and the births, it still came as a shock to find they were flesh and blood. He recognized Dolores's sister—Ruth?—but none of the other fifteen or so mourners. Just as well. The intensity of his grief would have made small talk—even commiseration—impossible.

To Pete's delight, Elizabeth, a lawyer, had risen from ten years with the U.S. Justice Department to become New Jersey's first female U.S. Attorney. Recently, she had uncovered major corruption in Monmouth County involving kickbacks by a contractor to mayors and assemblymen to assure his participation in a public housing project already behind schedule and running three times its estimated cost. Word was, Jake knew, that she was angling for governor, and he suspected she'd succeed. Her ambition and single-mindedness had scared him off when years ago they had dated briefly (Pete's idea); he supposed those attributes had only intensified. Markis, Jake guessed, didn't mind them. He was a high school football coach, affluent by inheritance and arrogant by nature, but, Pete had told him, "so much in her shadow it was sometimes tough to see him at all."

Elizabeth caught up to him on the church steps after the service and took him over to Markis and the kids. Markis was younger than Elizabeth, in his mid-thirties, Jake guessed, with thinning brown hair and dark eyes. His hostility toward Jake was badly disguised; he glared as though Jake were responsible for his father-in-law's death. *Probably hates me because I once went out with her. If I tell him all I got out of her was a kiss, and that an icy one, would he feel better?* Markis insisted on being called by his last name by anyone outside his family, his only pretension. Elizabeth didn't object—maybe, Jake guessed, because it made him sound important.

Elizabeth grabbed his arm. "Can I talk to you for a minute?" She was tall and thin and auburn-haired. Jake remembered how beautiful she was, but also how indifferent when they dated.

She led him up the stairs to the door of the church. "Elizabeth, I'm so sorry."

She bowed her head. "Thanks. I feel terrible that we didn't visit him more, but"—a rueful smile—"the kids are a handful, and I've been incredibly busy."

"So I read in the papers. No need to blame yourself. I didn't see enough of him, either."

"Still, I should have been a better daughter. It's not that his death wasn't expected. I mean, he had a heart condition and couldn't sit still for two seconds. I tried to talk him out of working. Fat chance."

"He was stubborn as hell."

"You said it." She blew her nose, took a step closer. "And on top of everything else . . . A couple of times when I called him at night, I could tell he'd been drinking. I hardly knew what was going on in my own father's life. Made me feel like a truant until Dad owned up."

"Cancer," Jake said, the word escaping too loudly.

"So Dad told you, too."

"No. I guessed. What kind was it?"

"Pancreatic. A death sentence. Incurable, inoperable, unbeatable."

Ah, Pete, you stoic bastard. I hope the rest of that scotch was ambrosia. He remembered something Harrigan always told his medical students before they entered the morgue for the first time: "It's the heart that animates life. When the murmur of the heart finally ceases, the rest remains silent." He wanted Pete to break his silence for one more day so he could tell him he loved him.

"Daniel and I drove up last Monday, after Dad and I had a heart-to-heart over the phone earlier that morning and he admitted he was sick. We had dinner with him. Daniel went back to New Jersey, and I stayed the night and had a federal marshal pick me up and take me to the office. He didn't seem particularly upset—said he knew his body and that something was very wrong. He spent most of the time telling us about the case he was working on, the one with the skeletons, and how you'd come to help. I can't tell you how thankful I am that I was there. It was the best talk we ever had." She squared her shoulders. "At least I got to see him. But I didn't think it was going to be this quick."

Jake felt a twinge of resentment. *Pete confides in his daughter but not in his best friend?* He put his hand on her back. "He had a good life and a long one. He got to see you that Monday night—you know how much he adored you—and then he worked until the last second, until the last breath."

"Actually, I don't know that he adored me, but I sure adored him." Elizabeth paused and jabbed at her eyes with a handkerchief. "You know how your friends say, 'Let me know if there's anything I can do?' Well, there's something *you* can do—if you don't mind."

The request came as a relief. "Name it."

"I can't face the cottage now. But somebody's got to go there. Dad's housekeeper, Mrs. Alessis, said vandals broke in over the weekend."

Rage made him light-headed. *What scum would do that?* "Anything missing?"

"Some of the liquor and pipe tobacco. Kids, probably."

"Still, what an awful thing to do." He was struck by his last image of Harrigan, glass in one hand, pipe in the other. Happy.

"The furniture's going to charity. The housekeeper said she'd stay on long enough to take care of it. But his study"—she shuddered—"he'd want you to have everything in it. His books, the bones and skulls, all those autopsy photos, God knows what else. You could take what you want when you go up there and leave the rest for a university or museum. Will you do it?"

He had no desire to see the place ever again. "Sure," he said. "I'd be glad to."

Jake knew he couldn't handle the job alone, and he needed Wally in the office to cover for him, so he conscripted his brother. Sam, Jake's only sibling, was seven years younger, but psychologically he remained a hippie; he lived in Greenwich Village, went to gallery openings and performance pieces, drank latte in cafés. He managed to hold on to a rent-stabilized apartment and a gaggle of artistic friends, though he was no artist himself. Unlike his friends, he didn't drink, smoke, or take dope, and he exercised religiously. On Saturday nights, a woman with a body by Dow Chemical slept by his side; Jake had never met the same one twice.

Sam had long prematurely gray hair and a body kept slender by years of yoga and tai chi. For a while, he'd returned to his Jewish roots, wearing a yarmulke and refusing to watch TV on the sabbath, but that had only lasted a matter of weeks. According to Jake, he never met a guru he didn't like. Whatever philosophy he had most recently latched on to was, he was convinced, the One True Way.

"What does he do?" people asked. This remained a mystery: Jake had no answer and Sam never told him. When Jake asked if they could drive upstate together, Sam was of course free. "It'll be centering," he said enthusiastically.

They got to the cottage around ten in the morning. There was a FOR SALE sign out front, the front door was open, and the curtains and much of the furniture were gone. "Mrs. Alessis," Jake called, "it's Jake Rosen. We spoke on the phone."

She came out of the bedroom, a woman in her sixties wearing a kerchief on her head and forty unnecessary pounds around the middle. Sam smiled at her as if she were a hot fudge sundae and he was the spoon. He looked at every female like that, Jake knew, whether she was nineteen or ninety-two.

"It's nice to meet you in person," Jake said. "I'm Jake Rosen, and this is my brother, Sam."

Sam tossed his ponytail. "Enchanted."

She smiled. "Can I get you boys some coffee?"

"We should get right to work," Jake said.

"Love some," said Sam. He was wearing a Diesel T-shirt and cargo pants.

Sam and Mrs. Alessis disappeared into the kitchen, and Jake retreated to the study. Melancholy overtook him as soon as he entered. Pete loved this room. Nothing seemed changed since the night he had found Pete's body; there were no telltale signs of the break-in. He swore Pete's spirit was *there.*

Shaking off gloom, Jake decided to tackle the books first, separating them into piles for himself, a university, the medical examiner's library, and the dump. His own pile grew rapidly. He had no idea where he was going to put everything.

"Sam," he called after an hour's work, "what are you doing out there?"

"Helping Theresa clean out the kitchen."

Theresa? "You're supposed to be helping me."

Sam stuck his head in the study door. "Chivalry is good karma."

Jake squinted at him. The dust from the books was starting to bother his eyes. "Do you ever listen to yourself talk?"

"All day long. What is it you want me to do?"

"You can start by getting me some boxes. As many as you can find."

Sam shrugged. "I'll go down to the liquor store. They always have boxes, right? We can treat Theresa to a glass of wine."

"You don't know where it is."

He looked hurt. "I'll figure it out."

Jake went back to work, feeling increasingly depressed. It wasn't just that it was hard to be surrounded by Harrigan's things, but he had barely made a dent in the books—he had found texts stretching back to Pete's high school science classes—much less the rest of the study. There had to be a dozen boxes filled with autopsy Kodachrome slides alone—and one, also containing jars and containers, had his name on it; he figured it dated back to the time the two had worked together—and there were the bones, the antique lab glass, the biological specimens in jars of formaldehyde. He'd just have to pile everything into boxes and go through it at home.

His own study in New York wasn't as cluttered as Pete's, but only because Jake had allowed it to spill over into the rest of the brownstone. Even his own bedroom was filled with books and files. If something happened to him, the job of clearing it would go to Sam. The thought terrified him.

Be careful you don't wake up in the morning, alone at the age of sixty, and regret the choices you made.

Harrigan's words. Did he have regrets when he died? Jake wondered. Probably.

There was a knock on the front door. "Mrs. Alessis? Can you get that?" No answer. He heard her vacuuming in one of the bedrooms.

Grumpily, he went to the door and opened it. Facing him was a woman in her fifties wearing black stretch pants and an embroidered floral sweater. She was painfully thin. Her timid smile revealed yellowed teeth; her hand, when she extended it, reminded him of a cat's claw. Fatigue lay deep in her sunken eyes, and her brunette hair was dyed and disheveled.

"Dr. Harrigan?"

"I'm sorry," Jake said. "I'm Dr. Rosen."

"Is Dr. Harrigan in?"

"No."

"I guess I should have called first. I'll wait. It's urgent."

"Was Dr. Harrigan a friend of yours?"

The question seemed to startle her. "No. I never met him before in my life."

A mystery. "I'm afraid he died recently."

She blinked at him. Jake thought she was going to cry. "Oh, no!" she wailed. "I need to talk to him about my father!"

Mystery no longer. "I see. Your father passed away. Dr. Harrigan did the postmortem?"

"I don't know what you call it," the woman said sullenly, as though blaming Jake for Harrigan's absence.

"Dr. Harrigan and I used to work together."

Her eyes lit up. "Then maybe you know what happened to my father. All I know is Dr. Harrigan found him—found his body."

"Found him?"

"Buried," she said, "in an unmarked grave."

"I'm Patrice Perez. My maiden name was Patrice Lyons. Daughter of James Albert Lyons."

With a shock, Jake remembered: Skeleton Three. Patient number 631217. Pete had located her. "Yes," he said, "I was with Dr. Harrigan when he found the remains." He led her to the kitchen and poured her a cup of coffee. "You hadn't seen your father, then, for several decades."

"I didn't know where he was. Dr. Harrigan's call was a thunderbolt. He told me I could stop by anytime and talk . . . about my dad . . . here or at the hospital. I came here first." She fiddled with the handle of her coffee mug. "I don't like hospitals."

There was steel underneath the frail façade, Jake realized. He was starting to like Patrice Perez. "How did Dr. Harrigan find you?"

"Through the Veterans Administration."

"Your father was in the military?"

"In Korea. He was an officer, a lieutenant," she said proudly. "Married Mom just before he went overseas. That's why he ended up in the looney bin."

Jake winced; he hated that term. "He suffered from post-traumatic stress?"

"Back then they called it shell shock. He saw his two best friends blown apart in front of him. Happened at a place called Heartbreak Ridge. I always thought that was a good name for it."

Heartbreak Ridge, Jake knew, was one of the bloodiest battles of the Korean War. "How long was he a patient?"

"Almost from the time he got back. He used to sleep with his helmet as a pillow. Had terrible headaches, sometimes violent seizures. I was about five. I remember him hitting his head against the wall and screaming."

Classic signs of epilepsy, Jake thought. She seems more composed now; it's helping her to talk.

"Mom had him hospitalized in December of sixty-three. He asked us not to come see him until he was better. We got letters from him from time to time. The last one was for me. He wrote that he'd had some type of surgery and was feeling better. But he didn't sign it like he did the rest: *You are my very own Pipsqueak, Love, Daddy.* Instead it was *Your father, Lieutenant James A. Lyons.*

"The letters stopped coming. When Mom called the hospital, they said he'd eloped." Her voice fell. "Wandered off and disappeared."

He wanted to embrace her, let her cry out her pain. "When was this?"

"Nine months later, in September of sixty-four. Mom thought maybe he'd started a new life, put his past behind him, but I wouldn't hear of it. 'He'd never leave without saying goodbye,' I told her. 'He loved me too much to do that.' "

Now the tears came, slowly at first, then in torrents. "I don't know what to do. I need to find out what happened to him. Mom died; I'm the only one left. Nobody cares about him except me. I tried to get his records, but the hospital's closed and the VA hardly has any medical files left. There was a fire, they told me, but maybe they were just saying that to get rid of me."

"No, it's true," Jake said. "I've come up against it before. It happened in St. Louis in 1973. A lot of VA records were lost."

He thought his answer would comfort her, but it seemed to deflate her further.

"I don't know what to do," she said again. "I have a daughter who deserves to know about her grandfather. But how am I to get a straight answer? I'm just a middle-aged divorced waitress from Jersey. To the government, I'm a big nobody."

Jake handed her a paper towel to dry her tears. "You could hire a private investigator."

She shook her head. "I don't have that kind of money. But I was wondering: what if it was the hospital's fault? Do you know a lawyer who might take my case?"

"You want to sue for damages?"

"I don't want *money*," she said, as though it were a four-letter word. "I just want to find out what happened to my father."

"You want an attorney willing to work for nothing—who'd take your case just for the satisfaction of finding out the truth?"

She sighed. "I know it's impossible."

"Actually," he said, "I know the perfect person for the job."

CHAPTER FOUR

WHEN SHE'D HEARD Jake's voice, Manny had hung up on him. When he'd called again, she acted more grown-up, finally admitting to herself that, arrogant as he was, he'd been right about Essie Carramia. She let him tell her about Patrice Perez. Then she called Patrice, whose story, like a familiar virus, infected her heart.

Now, somewhat to her surprise, Manny found herself in Poughkeepsie, New York, at the Psychoanalytic Academie for the Betterment of Life, a repository for the records of several now-defunct psychiatric hospitals, Turner among them. She'd surfed for Turner on the Internet and learned that New York State was paying the Academie to archive those of its records that were neither at the Turner Historical Society nor yet retrieved from the hospital itself. So, on a glorious fall day, she had put the top down on her convertible Porsche and driven up.

Manny had arrived before lunch, to give herself plenty of time to look at the files and drive back in the sunshine, though the building's gray exterior was like a dark cloud in the middle of the light. She entered its imposing iron-grated doors and walked up to a dour young woman with mousy shoulder-length hair sitting behind a mahogany desk bearing a black sign with gold lettering: RECEPTIONIST, PABL.

Manny smiled, knowing there was no way the woman would smile back. "Hi. I'm Philomena Manfreda. I called yesterday about records relating to the Turner Mental Hospital, later the Turner Psychiatric Institute."

The receptionist looked at her note pad. "Quite right. But Mr. Parklandius, our director, is still not in, and I'm not sure I can give you access to those items until he gets back." She squinted at Manny as though she'd left her glasses somewhere or the light was too dim.

She doesn't know who she's up against. Manny's smile broadened. "I'm sorry. I didn't catch your name?"

"Lorna Meissen. I'm Mr. Parklandius's assistant. It was I who spoke to you yesterday. I assumed he'd be in by now. Sorry about that."

"Lorna. Good morning. I didn't realize he had to be here in person. I thought the Academie functioned like a public library. I'm a lawyer, and the law says that since the library receives government funding, you can't deny me, a member of the public, access to the records. Mr. Parklandius would not have to give permission, so it doesn't matter whether he's here or not." *Do the new patient privacy laws really say that? If I don't know, it's a safe bet Lorna doesn't either.*

Lorna looked at Manny suspiciously. "I guess it'll be all right. I should warn you that the records might be hard to find. You're only the second person who's asked for them in my three years at the Academie." She stood. "Come. I'll take you upstairs to the reading room."

She locked the front door with a button from behind the desk and led Manny to an eerie old-fashioned open-cage elevator. The building was owned by the Hawkins family, she explained, who'd made their fortune in real estate. But no member of the family had ever visited, and Mr. Parklandius was closemouthed on the subject. As the elevator ascended, Manny noticed marble floors, vaulted ceilings, a sweeping staircase with a banister of polished brass.

They got off on the third floor. No one seemed to be in the building besides the two of them, Manny noted. She heard nothing but quiet. At the end of the hall on the right was a large room with several conference tables and uncomfortable chairs. The sign on its door read AUTHORIZED PERSONNEL ONLY. Across from it was a closed door with another sign: CHARLES P. PARKLANDIUS, DIRECTOR. Lorna settled Manny at one of the tables in front of a huge stack of file-bearing boxes, dated by year from 1888 to the present, which had evidently been laid out for her arrival. The hospital had been opened in 1869 as the Turner Home for the Feeble-minded, Lorna had told her, but these were the only files extant.

"I'll be downstairs," Lorna said. "I'm afraid if you need anything you'll have to come get me."

Manny watched her leave with relief. The room overlooked the Hudson River, and she could think of no more pleasant place to do her research in private. She picked up the first file, dated 1888, containing a list of names of people long dead and the treatments they received. The book could equally well have described the Dark Ages. It was embossed with a symbol, a circle that contained a star.

Other files contained more mundane records: an order for 150 sheets and pillowcases in 1916; prices paid for laboratory equipment in 1925; and—strange—a copy of the August 1963 *Baxter County Daily Gazette*. Unusual, Manny thought, for a newspaper to be included in medical files.

Ah. The front page was devoted to the upcoming Turner Mental Hospital summer picnic. A photograph of the grounds taken at a similar fête in May showed women strolling in spring dresses, men in fine suits at their sides. A schedule noted the time for the opening ceremonies and promised a barbecue, ring-tossing contest, square dance, and other social events. The public was invited to attend: admission $1 "for the benefit of indigent patients." There were several other photographs of the May event; some showed doctors, nurses, and patients posing with the patients.

It became clear to Manny that the Turner Mental Hospital, as it was called here, was more than a treatment center; it had been the social and economic core of Baxter County. Later files covered the final change of the hospital's name, a near drowning in its pool, a power failure, the menace of a rabid dog. And then, sadly, the closing of the institute due to lack of funds. GRIM DAY FOR TURNER, a headline in the hospital newsletter proclaimed.

Finally, Manny came to a different set of files: patients' records going back to the opening of the hospital. These she began to read with care, distracted from her search by accounts of the treatments for a variety of illnesses from dementia to alcoholism and how they changed over the years.

In all, Manny read for nearly five hours, spending just the last hour looking for the file on James Albert Lyons. She couldn't find his name, not in any of the years between the end of the Korean war and 1964, the day he disappeared. Maybe I've looked too quickly, she thought, and was about to start again when she felt more than heard Lorna Meissen creeping up behind her.

"I'm afraid you'll have to leave," Lorna said. "I'm the only one here, and I'm finishing up for the day."

Damn! "May I photocopy a couple of items?"

Lorna bridled. "I think you'll have to come back, Ms. Manfreda. I'm not sure photocopying's permitted."

Manny was too tired to invent a law to cover the situation. "Then may I have fifteen more minutes?"

"You may. But I leave at four-fifteen sharp."

Manny smiled at her. "Thanks. I'll be downstairs in a few." Indeed, she was already running late for her dinner date with Jake Rosen, and, having skipped lunch, she was famished.

When Lorna left, Manny rifled through the remaining files. She opened a cardboard cylinder labeled ARCHITECTURAL PLANS and stuffed it into her tote bag. None of the other files appeared to contain any information on the treatment of James Lyons. Manny justified her prospective action to herself. *It'll give me the feel of the place.* She added a variety of files that might contain information on James Lyons, though they didn't offer much hope. *I'll just take them home, look at them tonight, copy the ones I need in my office, and send them back. Lorna will be too terrified to tell her boss I took them, and no one else will miss this stuff for a few days—or a few years, for that matter.*

She repacked the boxes, left them on the table, and headed out the door, taking the stairs down. She'd have stopped at the second floor to snoop, but she didn't want to be late for Lorna. She heard the elevator rising as she reached the lobby and thought it was Lorna coming to look for her, but Lorna was waiting impatiently at the front desk. Perhaps the passenger was the mysterious Mr. Parklandius. Frustrated by the day, feeling she'd found nothing important, Manny fought the temptation to run back upstairs just to get a glimpse of him.

The air had turned cold. Manny put the top up on the Porsche and called her office.

"Dull day," her assistant, Kenneth, reported. "Nothing new on Cabrera or Morales. Mr. Williams claims whiplash. And, bless the good Lord, Mrs. Livingston finally sent you her check. We eat for another month, and don't forget the sale today at Bendel's."

Kenneth Medianos Boyd was a street kid who had earned his paralegal certification in jail. He dreamed of being a lawyer, but for that he needed a degree, and that meant money, which in turn necessitated two jobs: working for Manny and as a waitress named

Princess K in the nightclub Changing Places. Princess K, fastidious about the cleanliness of the ladies' room, printed out signs saying PLEASE MAKE SURE YOU FLUSH EVERYTHING DOWN THE TOILET and posted them in the stalls. He had been assigned to Manny as a pro bono client when he'd been arrested on charges of conspiracy to destroy evidence—drugs—by flushing it away. He spent the night in the men's lockup dressed in five-inch platform heels of shiny turquoise patent leatherette, a bright-green string bikini with ruffles and a tail of peacock feathers, full makeup, and, of course, shaved underarms. The men in the holding pen were terrified of him.

Manny didn't have to work hard to spring her client, despite his prior conviction on the same charges. The judge laughed so hysterically at the getup and the story he could barely gasp the words "Case dismissed." But they'd spent enough time together to bond. Kenneth was bright and hard-working, and he needed a day job. She could keep an eye on him and he could double as her fashion consultant, given his talent for mixing and matching outrageous clothes with shoes, bags, and scarves. Every day he checked the paper for designer sample sales.

"There's one thing more," he said. "Dr. Rigor Mortis called."

"You mean Rosen?"

"The very one. He's at a crime scene, wants to make your dinner later, suggests meeting you at six-thirty at the corner of Sixty-sixth and Third. Says you and he can talk about the case while you walk to the restaurant."

It'll give me time to change. What does one wear to get his attention, a death mask? "Call him back and tell him fine. And give him my cell phone number in case he's delayed again."

If he is, I wonder who'll do his autopsy.

It was dark when Manny got to the corner, but she could easily make out his slumped silhouette. He was standing under a street-light, poring over papers he had obviously extracted from the briefcase at his feet. *He* certainly hadn't gone home to change. His suit was wrinkled and he probably hadn't combed his hair since he testified at the Carramia trial.

She snuck up behind him. "Good evening."

Flustered, he put the papers away and faced her. "Ms. Manfreda, thanks for meeting me." He gawked. "Didn't you have red hair?"

"This week I'm blond," she said with a shrug. "Didn't want to clash with my new bag." She displayed a red tote, a valise-sized affair with natural leather trim and gold hardware. "It's a Vuitton. I was on the waiting list for nine months."

He stared at the bag, then at her. *What kind of lunatic . . . ?* An attractive one, he admitted. Her hair looked great, going nicely with the bag and her purple-and-red tweed suit. She had a full—*voluptuous*—figure, unlike the anorexics on TV and the streets of Manhattan, who all seemed in need of a big banana split. Her eyes were a shade between blue and gray, and her clear skin summoned up the usual comparison to porcelain. At least she didn't layer on the makeup. If he had learned one thing from the autopsy table, it was that too many women weren't content with the gifts nature had provided.

"See something interesting?" she asked.

He blushed, realizing he had stared too long and too hard. "I see what you mean about the bag and the hair."

"What restaurant are we going to?"

"Restaurant?"

"Yes. Kenneth told me you'd pick one and we'd discuss the case while we walked to it."

He picked up his briefcase. "Actually, I've no idea."

"My choice, then, Italian, of course," she said cheerfully. "Scalinatella. It's on Sixty-first between Third and Second."

"Fine." He started across the avenue.

"Wait! The WALK sign's blinking."

"There are no cars coming. Let's go."

She balked. "I don't run across streets, especially potholed streets, in shoes like these." She pointed to her four-inch heels.

"I'll hold you," he said. "You won't fall."

He took her right arm and led her in a half trot across Third Avenue. Her mind flashed to the time after his autopsy of Terrell when he'd shown her how the angle of a bullet track changes depending on the position of the shooter and the movement of the victim. "Terrell was standing," he'd said. "The shooter crouched on the ground behind him in the firing position the police are taught. That's what caused the upward angle. Here, let me show you." He'd put one hand on her back, the other on her chest above her right breast, and began to bend her body up and down slowly. "The most important thing, Ms. Manfreda, is that the bullet didn't hit the shoulder blade. We have two hundred and six bones in the human body. The only bone that moves up and down on the other bones is the shoulder blade—the scapula. Terrell's shoulder blade was up when he was shot, which means his arm was over his head in surrender like the neighbors said, and he was not going for a gun in his pocket as the police claimed."

Now, rushing across the avenue, what Manny remembered was not the words, though they had freed her client, but the feel of his hands, which sent a tingle down her spine because she thought she might do something silly, like turn around and kiss him. *Madness.*

They stepped onto the curb. Jake gestured toward a white brick building across the avenue. "That's where Tennessee Williams died. Choked on a bottle cap, according to the autopsy report. His brother never believed it, claimed Williams was murdered. I reviewed the files. The brother was partially right. The bottle cap didn't kill him. He died of a drug and alcohol overdose. It wasn't murder."

Impressive. "Weren't we supposed to talk about the Lyons case?"

"It can wait. See that streetlamp on the next corner? That's where Benjamino Bellincaso bought it. *Bang!* Killed by a gunman who disappeared into the subway. Started a Mafia war that went on for years. Used to be a famous steakhouse there, but they had to move. Nobody wanted to eat at the site of Bellincaso's last supper."

"Anything else on this sightseeing tour I should know about?" *I shouldn't have asked.*

"There was another restaurant near here, the Neapolitan Noodle, forced to close because four garment company executives were shot at a table some organized crime people had just left. Nobody found out who the intended victims were."

He was still holding her arm; she made no effort to dislodge it. The passion in his voice, his stride, and his expression were infectious. She felt comfortable with him, mesmerized.

"Normal people don't navigate by crime scenes," she said, when at last he paused for breath. "Have you ever been to Bloomingdale's? It's three blocks away. Great store, fabulous clothes, and *two* shoe departments, one for the times a woman wants to feel chic, the other when she wants to dress like a diva."

"Really? I didn't know." A monotone.

She pressed on. "Women navigate by stores—live by them. Shopping, fashion, and clean ladies' rooms with soft toilet paper." *He's a doctor. He can take anatomic information.* "On the far side of Bloomie's there's an outlet store. I bought my Hermès scarf and coordinating enamel bracelets at their warehouse sale at the end of the year. It's when they mark down their dated products, but with Hermès, who cares? After all, my Kelly bag is timeless."

He's staring at me again. Does he think I've gone out of my mind? No, he was smiling. Indeed, his eyes were lit by what she took to be enjoyment. "Here's Scalinatella," she said. "Their specialty is rare, juicy steak and lobster fra diavolo pasta misto, but after all that spilled blood in the restaurants around here, I think I'll have fish."

CHAPTER FIVE

"*BUONA SERA*," said Manny, as they followed the maître d' to a corner table.

Jake took off his blue blazer, loosened his maroon-and-black print tie below the fraying collar of his light-blue button-down shirt, and rolled up his sleeves—*as though he's about to begin an autopsy*—all before he sat down across from her.

"Do you care for wine?" their waiter asked. They each reached for the wine list. A tug of war ensued, which Manny won.

"Red or white?" she asked.

"Your choice."

She assessed the offerings. "We'll have the ninety-five Amarone—the Reserva Ducale, *piacere*."

The waiter bowed. "Good choice. And your accent"—he kissed his fingers—"impeccable."

"I'm second-generation Italian."

"And a bottle of mineral water, with gas," Jake told the waiter.

She squinted at him. "How very European."

There was still an edge to her voice; Jake wasn't sure if she was mocking him.

He filled her glass when the sparkling water arrived.

They were on dessert and espresso. When they'd arrived, Jake, rather than the maître d', had pulled out her chair for her, a bit of old-fashioned gallantry she found charming. He'd also ordered sea bass for them both and talked virtually nonstop about violent death.

"Now, about the Lyons case," Jake finally said. "I think—"

"Yes, *about* the Lyons case," she interrupted. "Just what *were* you thinking?"

Jake raised an eyebrow. "Excuse me?"

"I don't hear from you between Terrell and Carramia—and after Carramia not so much as an apology after you crucified me. Then you call to tell me a woman I've never met is about to contact me so I can represent her because you think I'm a great lawyer." Her eyes narrowed. "Was that supposed to be a joke?"

"I can see why it might seem a little odd. But you really impressed me in court, and when Mr. Lyons's daughter—"

"You'll say anything, won't you? Anything to get your way. I impressed you in court? How can you say that with a straight face? You made me look like an undergrad."

He smiled without condescension. "An impressive undergrad, then. Look, I'm a scientist. I'm hired to give an opinion based on science, and that opinion's what it is, no matter who asks for it. I didn't testify against you, I testified against false conclusions. Just as I wasn't hired to testify *for* you in the Terrell case. If the police hadn't shot your client in the back, I'd have told you so."

Okay, he's not for sale. But he's still smug. The spoon bearing a bite of tiramisu stopped halfway to her mouth. When he'd opened his collar and rolled up his sleeves before they'd sat down, she'd thought it bad manners; now his casualness and ease, his obvious sincerity and the frankness of his gaze opened a gate in her brain, and she let him enter.

"You'd been given some wrongheaded opinions," he went on. "But beyond that you were better prepared than any attorney I've ever seen. Digging up that study I did on witness accounts in police takedowns—amazing. And you're obviously very . . . zealous in representing your clients' interests. I've read up on some of your cases. You got a record settlement in the Terrell case when nobody else wanted to touch it. And when the governor refused to issue a permit to those anti–death penalty protesters, you headed the First Amendment challenge. That was an elegant brief you wrote, by the way." He lunged across the table to grab her hand. "Watch out. The tiramisu's about to drop on your jacket."

She swallowed it. "You bet I care about my clients. I didn't traipse up to Poughkeepsie for you, I did it for Patrice Perez. And if I find out this is some sort of scam, I'll roast her till she's tender."

"Scam? No way. You haven't met her. If there was ever a more vulnerable, more—"

"Forgive me, Dr. Rosen, but I've found that scientists know little about the human heart. Vulnerable is a con artist's stock-in-trade."

"You think she's a con artist?"

"I didn't say that. Just mentioned the possibility."

She's trying to one-up me, Jake thought. Pay me back. The idea pleased him. "Still, you traipsed up to Poughkeepsie."

"Of course. If she's straight, the poor woman thought her father abandoned her. Now she has no idea what happened to him. For all she knows, the doctors in that psycho ward botched his treatment and buried him in the backyard like a mad dog." She sipped her wine, though all the talk of death and destruction made her want to chug it back. "Even if there's no wrongdoing here, the State of New York still owes her an explanation. She may not have fifty dollars in the bank, but she has every right to stand up for her—" She cut herself off. "What are you smiling about?"

"You really care. I like that."

She shrugged. "My father nicknamed me Saint Jude after the patron saint of lost causes."

"I see." He took a bite of his warm chocolate cake. "But he named you Philomena Erminia."

They looked at each other, eyes lingering for a moment. "Found out my middle name, did you?"

"I'm very thorough," he said. "Besides, it was on the court records."

She digested that for a second. "Now we're on the same team, you might as well call me Manny. Everybody does."

"Not Philly?"

"Not," she said, "if you want to keep your teeth."

They ordered more coffee. She told him about her trip to the Academie and how fruitless it seemed to her. "Interesting about the hospital's history, but not a word about Lyons."

"Maybe that's interesting in its own way. Significant."

"It *is* strange. There are files for other patients from around the same time. His is missing."

"Stolen, you think? Destroyed?"

"Could be. Patrice said you found the remains. You and a Dr. Harrigan, who seems to have since died. Anything significant about them?"

He wondered if she was mocking him, but her tone and expression were serious. The sparring they had engaged in earlier had ceased in the face of their mutual cause. "Lots," he said. "For one thing, we made a positive identification through the dental records. But you already know about that."

"What about the cause of death?"

"Fracture of the second cervical vertebra."

"The hangman's break."

"O-ho! How did you know about that?"

"The history of lynching intrigues me. I'm a collector of those moments when the courts have bestowed their imprimatur on the immoral. Keeps me from being too reverent about our legal system—as if I ever was." She leaned forward. "How can you be sure his neck didn't break when the body was dumped into the grave?"

"Because when we looked under the microscope we saw iron, the residue of broken-down hemoglobin. That means there was bleeding at the fracture site, which in turn means—"

"That he was alive when it happened. Do you think he could've been hanged?"

"It's possible. But given that he was in a mental hospital, I think there's a likelier explanation. The broken neck could be a consequence of electroshock therapy."

She shuddered involuntarily. "Brutal."

"Years ago, if they used too much current and didn't administer a muscle relaxant—or the staff wasn't trained right—it happened. I can show you examples in the museum at the ME's office."

"I'll pass." She swirled her tiny spoon in the espresso cup. "What gets me is that no one cared about his death. The court system only worries about statistics, how many cases the judge has closed."

He shared her cynicism. Careless autopsies, sloppy evidence, false testimony—these had always influenced courts, which didn't seem to give a damn when the errors were discovered. *Case closed* all too often meant *case closed forever.* "Look," he said, "you and I know this wasn't a natural death. It should have been reported to the medical examiner, but it wasn't. It should have been reported to Lyons's wife, but it wasn't."

"Do you think the legal system's concerned about truth, justice, and fairness? In my experience—*no!*" Manny's voice was so loud the kissing couple at the next table stopped to look at her.

"We're not done yet. I haven't even seen the X-rays. Dr. Harrigan's secretary was supposed to forward them to me, but they haven't arrived. I'm not sure what's taking so long."

"What about toxicology?"

"Harrigan was going to use an outside lab. Haven't seen the paperwork, though."

"Why didn't Harrigan let the hospital lab deal with it?"

"Because he didn't trust them. Regular hospital labs are notoriously bad at toxicology. They're set up to do testing of normal body chemistry; it stops there."

She pushed back her espresso cup. "In the meantime, I'll try to run down Lyons's medical records. Maybe they overlooked some in the hospital before it closed. And I'll see if I can find anybody who knew him, in the hospital or before. Maybe some of his army buddies are still alive. I can also try to talk to the doctors who treated him, if I can find out who they are. Patrice will waive the medical privilege."

He looked at her sympathetically. "You should hire an investigator. You must be busy."

"I can't afford one. Losing Carramia wasn't pretty for me. I spent a lot of money on that case, and when you lose it doesn't get refunded. And new clients don't start running your way, either. Thank God for the Terrell settlement. Without it, I'm reduced to last year's clothes. "

Jake shifted uncomfortably. *I won't say I'm sorry she lost.* "I can pay for a private investigator, if it would help."

Manny thought she'd been reduced to a third-grader in Catholic school, sitting in front of her stern teacher, her hands folded in front of her. *I guess you can afford it when you bill five* grand for a day, she thought, her sassiness trumping softness. "Thanks, but I'd just as soon do it myself."

"You're really going up to Turner Hospital? It's a dreadful place. Better take someone with you."

But not you. You're *too busy.* She felt resentment return like nighttime and stood, anxious to get home.

His cell phone rang, and he motioned her down. "I'll be right back." The caller ID said it was from upstate. He moved toward the bar.

Manny sat in his chair and rummaged through his jacket pockets. There were car keys, house keys, a quarter and a penny, a roll of Tums, and a letter from a woman that her conscience didn't let her read. *Maybe he does spend time with people who still have a pulse.*

She retreated to her own seat, wondering if she should have tried to work things out with Alex, whom she had dated for a year. He was a banker with a self-involvement that often left her a bystander, but kind nevertheless. He had wanted to marry her, but he had also wanted her to "leave the trial work to others," so that was that.

Jake returned. He tried a smile, but it was obvious that he was troubled.

"What's wrong?" she asked. "You look freaked out."

"I've been called upstate to do an autopsy. There's no medical examiner, and the family asked for me."

Turner, she thought, and felt a spasm of foreboding. "Who died?"

"Dr. Harrigan's housekeeper," he said soberly, gazing at the wall.

"Dinner's on me," Manny said, reaching for her credit card. "Patrice is my client; protocol dictates I pay."

His own card materialized. "My mother taught me never to let a lady pay for dinner. *She* dictates who pays."

Charming. Fashion-challenged, but a courtier. "My turn next time," she said feebly, not sure that, after the Vuitton bag, there was room for another hundred-dollar charge on her account. *If there is a next time.* He paid. They stood.

"I'll escort you home," he said, "then head out to Turner."

"Now?"

"Her family sounded desperate." His voice was weary. "Corpses don't seem to care about time. And the sooner you get to them, the more you can find."

I don't want him to leave. The thought, unbidden and unexpected, stunned her. "I'll drive," she said.

He struggled to put on his jacket. One hand seemed to be stuck in the sleeve. He stared at her. "What are you talking about?"

"Turner. I'm coming with you."

"Impossible."

"Really? Try to get rid of me."

He thought for some moments. She waited for his answer, surprised by her own anxiousness. "Okay."

Is he humoring me or does he actually want me with him? No matter. "Good. We'll take my car."

"A Porsche! For a woman who lost the Carramia case, isn't it a bit extravagant?" They were in the parking garage near the restaurant. She didn't tell him the car was "previously owned."

"I bought it before Carramia. I do win, and sometimes win big, from time to time," she said. "And besides, clothes and cars aren't extravagances." She decided not to explain her mother's philosophy.

He held out his hand for the keys. She looked at it. "You've got to be kidding."

"I should drive."

"You may have failed to notice," she said, "but this is my car. Besides, you're in no condition to drive. You had two glasses of wine."

He rubbed his temple; she was giving him a headache. "Two hours ago. I'm a male weighing a hundred and ninety-five pounds who just ate a full meal. Would you like me to explain the metabolism rate of alcohol in the human body?"

"God, no!"

"Fine. Then give me the keys. We've got to drive up there, do the post, then come back to the city. There's no sticking to the speed limit."

She gave him the keys. He slid into the driver's seat. "Where's the damn ignition?"

She held back a laugh. "To the left of the steering wheel, exactly where it belongs in a Porsche Cabriolet, in homage to its racing-car roots."

He looked down. "Shit. It's got three pedals."

The laugh exploded. "Of course. It's a *Porsche.*"

He got out of the car and handed her the keys. "I don't drive a stick," he said.

She thought of a dozen nasty comebacks but didn't share them. *What man under eighty can only drive an automatic?*

They zoomed out of the garage, crosstown, then stopped in front of a building. "What's the matter?" he asked. "Don't know how to drive a stick?"

She glared at him. "I can't leave my baby alone all night. Watch the car."

"Baby?" he yelled after her, but she was already gone.

He waited in the car while she went up to her apartment. Had she ever mentioned a baby? He pictured himself trying to help a crazy woman buckle a child's car seat into the Porsche. Was she seriously intending to bring an infant to a postmortem? Why did I agree to let her come? he asked himself, but he did not attempt an analysis.

She returned, carrying a bundle and a tote bag. "What took you so long?" he asked.

"Mycroft needed a walk around the block." She took her place at the wheel and deposited the bundle in his lap.

It moved. "A poodle!" *She's certifiable.*

"Just one year old. I can't leave him for most of the night. He likes to be held."

"You've got to be—"

"And could you roll down your window? Mycroft likes fresh air."

She passed him the tote—Prada—filled to bursting. He tried to find space on the floor for both it and his feet, knowing which she'd insist had preference.

"What the hell have you got in here?"

"Some catch-up reading to do while you hack up the body. Most of it is for Mycroft: his security blanket, toys, bowl, Evian, and bully stick; his fleece, in case it gets cold; his favorite little red pillow. You know—the basics."

"You carry a bottle of spring water for your dog?" Jake and Mycroft eyed each other. The animal's coat was shiny and neatly clipped, but his lower jaw jutted out oddly, a tooth skewing to one side. "Hell of an underbite," he said. "And the hair around his mouth makes him look like he just ate a doughnut."

"He's too young for an orthodontist. But I'll have you know Mycroft's an entrepreneur. His groomer named a perfume after him: Mycroft Millefleurs, Parfum for the Precious Pooch." She looked directly at him. "All men should be so lucky."

———

They reached Baxter Community Hospital in under two hours, which Jake filled by telling her about Pete Harrigan and the cancer that took his life. When they arrived, Jake went right to the morgue, leaving Mycroft in the car with his favorite chew toy and a bowl of spring water and depositing Manny in the adjacent waiting room, intended for families brought to identify their loved ones. It was a depressing little room, with flickering fluorescent lights and no windows. Manny felt her excitement disappear, replaced by the grim reality of death and sorrow. She wondered how a man like Jake could spend his life facing it. What tragedies had he seen? How did he defend himself against them? Death from old age usually requires no autopsy, she knew. So the deaths Jake contemplated were homicides, suicides, accidents—lives cut short. She had seen a few dead bodies in her work and often felt she was their champion. But to *handle* them, to dwell on them? Unthinkable.

"Manny?"

She nearly jumped from her couch. "Jake! You scared me. Finished so soon?"

"Haven't started. There's no diener."

"Diener?"

"Autopsy assistant. Moves the body, sews it up when the ME's finished, helps with the stuff in between." The skin under his eyes was gray with fatigue. "I just got off the phone with the coroner in the next county over. He's running things here since Pete . . . since there's no Baxter County ME. He said the regular diener's out of town and they can't track down the backup man."

"How long till they find him?"

He gave her a small smile. She hoped it was meant to be charming.

"Actually—"

She knew what was coming next.

CHAPTER SIX

MANNY HAD NEVER been to a live autopsy. It was the fitting end for a day in which she was dressed to kill. She was head-to-toe Chanel, even her scarf. The outfit was so chic Coco herself would die for it—again. She had never considered herself a "girlie" girl. Since her parents had only one child, her Italian father had raised her like a son. She had learned to fish, throw dice and a football, and fix her own electrical outlets. She liked martial arts, James Bond, and Saturday afternoon monster flicks. When she was little, her father had taught her to play in the sandbox with the boys; now she competed in a rather larger arena.

"Theresa Alessis's daughter found Theresa lying dead on the kitchen floor and called an ambulance," Jake explained. "The paramedics tried CPR. Useless. They telecommunicated with the emergency-room doctor, who pronounced her dead, and brought the body here. Nobody's touched her since. If this were the city, the diener would've taken her out of the body bag, removed her clothes, and prepared her for autopsy. Here, she's still in the body bag. Since we don't know what happened to her, we have to do the examination carefully."

He led her through the morgue door, which swung shut behind them.

"Oh my God!"

The autopsy room was far smaller than the one Jake was used to, but it had the same look. A metal table stood in its center, the foot end over a sink and a black body bag on top of it, one that was clearly inhabited. Two white body bags, equally occupied, lay on stretchers against the wall.

"What's the matter?" Jake asked.

"There are dead people in those bags, just lying around."

He gave her a look. "It's a morgue."

"And that smell!"

"Formaldehyde used to preserve biological specimens."

"It's awful. Is it safe?"

"Some people think it can cause cancer. I've been breathing it for twenty years, and it hasn't done me any harm yet."

"But have you tried to have children?"

Another look. "Very funny. Let's check on the body." He grasped the zipper pull of the black body bag, which bore a heavy paper tag that read ALESSIS, THERESA, along with an identification number. "Right corpse. Time for us to get changed."

"How come those other bodies are in white bags?" Manny asked.

"White's used in hospitals up here. The bodies are probably waiting to be shipped to a funeral home. They won't be autopsied. Come with me."

They left the room and went a few doors down the hall to a small locker room, where he handed her a set of green surgical scrubs. "Put these on. We can change behind the lockers. I won't peek if you won't."

She eyed them, shapeless things that looked like pajamas from a prison camp. "No way."

"Trust me," he said. "You'll be glad you did."

"Can't I just put something over my suit, like an apron?"

"You don't want to do that."

"Don't tell me what I want to do." *Petulant. Unbecoming. Who cares? Anything to delay going back into that room.*

"Fine." He handed her what looked like a white plastic kimono, with cropped sleeves and a hem that went to her ankles. "One size fits all," he said.

She rolled up her $2,000 sleeves so they wouldn't appear beneath the plastic and then donned her armor. He wound the plastic belt around her waist, tying it snugly at the back. The gesture felt oddly intimate.

"Manny, are you there?" He waved his hand in front of her face. "You're supposed to faint when we cut the body open, not before."

"Sorry. I was thinking about—" She stopped in the nick of time.

He gave her a pair of blue paper booties. "Wear these, unless you don't mind having those shoes spattered with blood and other body fluids."

Blood? Body fluids? Her slingbacks—twin four-inch-high works of art in multicolored red suede with contrasting purple and red-checked pony-skin heels—deserved better.

"You don't want to go tramping blood and bacteria over your living room rug," he added, eyes twinkling. *The son of a bitch is having fun. He's enjoying himself. I hate him!* Her stomach acted up. The tiramisu that had tasted so delicious going down was on the verge of coming up.

He changed into scrubs and she followed him back into the autopsy room, girding for the moment when he exposed the corpse. Apparently, though, he had some setting up to do. He pulled over a small metal table holding a square of brown corkboard and arranged an assortment of instruments: clamps, knives, forceps, oddly shaped scissors, scalpels, extra blades, rulers, and a soup ladle.

"That looks like a steak knife," she said, pointing to an instrument with a wooden handle and a six-inch blade.

Jake grinned. "I had a colleague who gave two of them he took from an autopsy room to his wife as an anniversary present."

"How romantic. Didn't he ever hear of Tiffany's—little blue box, pretty white ribbon?"

He handed her a pair of latex gloves. "Put these on. And this." It was a paper face mask. *Goodbye, makeup.* His gloves and mask were already in place.

"Isn't this primitive for you?" she asked. "You must be used to all sorts of fancy equipment in the city."

"It's not much different in the city. MEs have been using the same instruments for a hundred and fifty years, ever since autopsies were made legal. And I'd rather work in a place like this than in a modern building, where you can't see a darn thing. Somehow the ceiling lights are never over the autopsy tables."

He strode to the table and unzipped the body bag. Manny took a step back. The corpse wore floral pajamas. Jake gently removed the clothing intact. Manny felt gooseflesh on her arms. Theresa Alessis lay completely naked now. Her mouth was ajar, her skin drying. Not a body that had been prettied with makeup and posed in a facsimile of sleep, as in a funeral home.

Manny felt a wave of sadness. Mrs. Alessis seemed pathetic, a hunk of sagging skin. No one in her right mind would ever want to be so diminished, so exposed. I'd best die in my sleep, she thought. No autopsy, please. She made a mental note to go back to the gym. "My God," she said. "The smell!"

"It gets to everybody at first," Jake said. "You'll be fine."

"It's like rotten eggs, only worse."

"Decomposition; the human body breaking down. Corpses emit intestinal gases such as hydrogen sulfide. It's a natural process—from ashes to ashes. God's way of recycling."

"Very comforting. I'm a lawyer, Dr. Rosen. I'm supposed to be lawyering. I do not belong in this morgue. I want to go home!"

He was smiling. *Enjoy yourself. Have a good time. Torture Manny. What fun.* She expected a lecture on why she should have changed into scrubs, but all he said, very politely, was, "If you want, I'll put some VapoRub inside your mask. It'll cover the smell. Ever since *The Silence of the Lambs,* when Jodie Foster used it, half the cops and DAs slather it under their noses at postmortems. I think the effect's more psychological than physical."

"No. Thanks. If you don't mind, I'll just sit for a minute."

"Sure." He indicated a chair. Meanwhile, he pulled a metal stool next to the autopsy table and used it as a step to haul himself up so he stood straddling the corpse. Then he took a camera and began shooting photos of the body. "When I attended my first autopsy, the ME had a cup of coffee in one hand and was poking through the decedent's organs with the other. Disgusting! I couldn't understand how someone could be so callous and insensitive. A half-dozen autopsies later, I was doing the same thing."

"That's a charming story," she said. "Thank you for sharing."

"I was trying to make you feel better." He got down, turned the body over, and climbed back for another round of pictures. "I'll need your help now."

She rose wobbily to her feet. "At your service." *You monster.*

He retrieved a long wooden stick from the corner of the room and handed it to her. "Align the bottom to the heel, then measure the height at the top of the head." He picked up a notebook and pen. "What's the measurement?"

She stood with the ruler and tried not to look at the body. "Um . . . sixty-four inches."

"Weight?"

"God knows. Am I supposed to guess?"

"That's how it's done. If there's no body scale, we estimate."

"That's crazy. Okay . . . I'd say one hundred sixty-five and a half pounds."

"Very good. My thought exactly, though it's hard to tell about that half pound. Maybe it's the Krispy Kreme she had for breakfast. When we open the stomach—"

"Please!" *Sadist.* "Do you get the weight wrong a lot of the time?"

"We do, for various reasons. But the most disputed statistic is height. Family members read an autopsy report and swear it isn't their relative. Know why?"

"Because people lie about how tall they are?"

"Right. Studies of drivers' licenses show people—especially short people—often add inches to their height." He handed her the pad and pen. "Now, a sample of the vitreous humor of the eye." He picked up a syringe.

"Wait!" Manny screamed. "You're going to stick that thing into her eye?"

"You bet. The fluid in the white part of the eye can tell us time of death as well as toxicology. We'll take some from both eyes and put it in two separate test tubes. Notice that the eyes are jaundiced."

She turned her back. "Tell me when you're done."

"Finished," he said, half a minute later. "Next, the external examination. To a forensic pathologist, the skin is the body's most important organ." He ran his fingers over the body. "We look for signs of injury—gunshot wounds, stab wounds, blunt trauma. In the case of Mrs. Alessis, none. There's no apparent bruising, no injury to the neck that could indicate strangulation. Write that down, please."

She realized Jake was easing her discomfort by teaching her as he worked, but her feeling of gratitude disappeared with his next words.

"Help me turn her onto her side and hold her steady."

"*Me?*"

He looked around the room. "I don't see another diener."

I'll diener you. Manny put down her notebook. The woman's skin felt icy, even through the latex gloves. Although she knew logically that dead flesh would be cold, she had unconsciously expected it to feel like living tissue. *But it feels like death itself.* She was only able to hold on by fixing her gaze on the big institutional clock on the morgue wall. *One-thirty. Mycroft and I should be in bed.*

"Lividity along the back and the backs of the legs and neck shows that the red blood cells settled while she was lying on her back after she collapsed," he said, demonstrating by pressing on the skin as he spoke. "Lividity is nonblanching. It's not really an issue here, but it indicates she died more than eight to ten hours ago."

"Nonblanching?"

"If you press on it, the maroon color doesn't fade." He reached for her hand. "I'll show you."

She looked away. "I believe you."

"There's an old autopsy adage: 'You watch one, you do one, then you teach one.' "

"There's another old saying, one you should be familiar with: 'Not over my dead body.' "

He didn't laugh. *No sense of humor.* "Let her down now, very gently. Thank you."

She eased the body onto its back again, thankful for the gloves—not much, but better than nothing.

"Keep writing," he told her. "Shame I couldn't find a tape recorder. She has a lot of dark hair on her arms and legs. I want to check for puncture wounds from a needle, make sure a new suitor didn't kill her by injection." He put a new blade on the scalpel handle and shaved the hair from the underside of her forearms, particularly near the bend of the elbows. Then he moved to her legs, her varicose veins revealed as the hair fell away.

He handles the scalpel masterfully. Not a nick. What would it feel like if he shaved my *legs?* She hoped he didn't see her blush. *Temporary insanity due to chemical intoxication. Let's not take this any further.*

"Not a pinprick," Jake said. "We move to the internal examination."

Goody.

He put a new blade on the handle. "We must evaluate the internal organs. That means taking them out." He reached for the body, hesitated. "You can step out for a moment if you need some air. Sometimes first-timers faint, but it's always the men, never the women."

She thought of the sandbox. *Damned if I'll be the first.* "I'm fine." She knew how unconvincing she sounded. *Even the corpse doesn't believe me.* "Go ahead."

With the slightest pressure, he cut across the upper left chest and shoulders, curved the scalpel under the breasts to the right shoulder, and continued down to the lower abdomen just to the left of the belly button.

"It's called a **Y**-incision."

"I'd never have guessed."

The thin cut widened almost instantly as the skin pulled apart, revealing a ravine of flesh and fat. Manny forced herself to watch, trying not to hyperventilate as Jake's scalpel sliced through layers of pale skin, glistening yellow fat, and pink muscle. *He's peeling poor Mrs. Alessis open like an orange.* A few small rivulets of blood ran down the sides of the corpse into the holes in the autopsy table.

"Some people believe that dead bodies don't bleed," Jake explained. "But when we die our vessels are filled with blood and will leak if they're cut, just like a garden hose leaks water."

He pulled out a handheld electric saw and turned it on.

"Yikes!" The sound was like a dentist drill magnified a thousand times.

Jake, though, seemed unperturbed as he cut through the breastplate to get at the internal cavities. He looked up as he cracked the breastplate away from the skin incisions. "Are you all right?"

She knew she had gone pale. Her uncovered shoes were dotted with blood. "I think I'll take that VapoRub now."

He motioned to the jar, and she took off her gloves to wipe a glob under her nose. "Put on new gloves," he said. She obeyed.

Jake was holding Mrs. Alessis's heart in his hands, raising it for her to see. "The heart is just a muscle," he said. "It's a pump. The lungs are the bellows. The kidneys are the plumbing. The skeleton is the scaffolding. The stomach and small intestines are the furnace, turning fuel—food and water—into energy. The liver, gallbladder, urinary bladder, kidneys, and large intestines are the sanitation department; they get rid of waste. And the brain—ah, the wonder of it!—is a high-powered computer so sophisticated that other brains don't begin to understand it."

"Fascinating," she croaked. *Don't faint. Don't vomit. Pretend you're paying attention.*

"I've never been a religious man," he went on, "especially considering the horrors I see, day in, day out: the dead children, the victims of violence, the awful waste of life. But when I look inside the human body, I can understand why people believe in a grand design. It's an awesome machine, don't you think?"

"You are so right."

"Heart's of normal size." He took a blood sample to be sent to toxicology. "Lungs pink and healthy. She wasn't a smoker." Jake removed the organs from the body and weighed them, the quickest way, he said, to tell if they were normal. The image of the bloody organs hanging from the scale prompted another round of nausea. *I'm never going inside a butcher shop again.*

"Next, the head," he said cheerfully.

Uh-oh.

He sliced the scalp from ear to ear and peeled the skin forward over the face. Then he fired up the electric saw, cut open the skull plate, and loudly cracked it back to reveal the brain, which he pulled out and sliced into cutlet-sized pieces.

"They say lawyers don't have brains," Manny managed. *And without question, medical examiners have no hearts.*

Two hours later, the autopsy was over. Washed and doused with perfume but still feeling sick, Manny ventured outside. This is what paradise feels like, she thought, and filled her lungs with the nectar of the night. In her mind she retained the vision of Jake opening Mrs. Alessis's stomach and ladling—yes, ladling!—its soupy contents into a plastic container. She reminded herself that he was simply trying to determine the cause of the woman's death, to give her family some peace of mind. But how could a man spend his life routinely cutting up corpses? She'd never witnessed anything so barbaric. *If he ever touched me, I'd remember the ladle and the heart. I'll bet he's still a virgin.*

Jake joined her, still wearing his scrubs. "There you are!" he said. "I have to go to the pathology lab. Want to come with me or stay out here?" He brandished a glass jar.

She pointed to it. "What's in that thing?"

"Part of Mrs. Alessis's liver." His tone was serious, his expression troubled. "It's wrinkled and underweight. Important, given the yellowish color of her eyes."

"For the record," Manny said, "I'm sorry I asked."

"So you coming with me or not?"

She listened to the sounds of the night. The crickets were out in full force, and she thought she heard an owl. *Creepy.* "With you."

She followed him to the pathology lab, where he headed to a machine the size of a microwave and switched it on. "It's for making frozen sections. Works in a matter of minutes. During surgery, for example, you use it to make sure you've removed enough of a cancerous organ. Normally, I'd wait for the permanent slides made from the paraffin blocks, but that takes a couple of days and I want to look at this tonight."

Something was bothering him. His demeanor was grim, perplexed. "Why?"

"I think the cause of death is related to the liver. There's her jaundice, the fact that the liver's wrinkled and underweight—a thousand grams instead of the normal twelve hundred fifty or so. But the only way to pinpoint the cause is to look at the liver under a microscope, and I want to do it before we leave." Jake inserted the liver section in the machine.

"I guess I still don't understand." Struck by his manner, she realized there were to be no more jokes. "Why do her kids feel so strongly about an autopsy? Do they think she was killed?"

"First off," he said, "the next of kin can request a private autopsy, even if the authorities don't think it's necessary."

"That doesn't answer the question."

"Actually, I doubt if Mrs. Alessis's children would have thought of it if she hadn't been smitten with my brother, Sam. He talked me up to her; she told her kids about my work. Voilà."

The machine beeped. He carefully cut a thin sliver of tissue from the frozen block of liver tissue, as though it were deli meat. "This is called a microtome blade," he explained. "It's very sharp. I'll put the tissue section on a slide, add some dye, put a cover slip over it, and it's ready to go." He inserted the slide under the microscope and adjusted the focus. After a minute he stood, that same troubled expression in his eyes. "Here. Take a look for yourself."

"I'm fine right where I am."

"Don't be a baby, you've been through an autopsy. This is just a slide. Besides, I may need you as a corroborating witness."

That did it. She felt a surge of excitement, even pleasure, and put her eye to the microscope. "What am I looking for?"

"You see those pink pie-shaped areas? They're called the liver lobules. Normally, under this stain each cell nucleus is blue, surrounded by pink cytoplasm."

"But some of them—"

"Are a mess." His voice was hoarse. He was pacing now, clearly fighting to keep his emotions under control. "You can see where the nuclei have been destroyed. It's dead tissue, what we call necrotic. Because it's in the center of the liver, we refer to this kind of damage as centrilobular necrosis."

"And what does it mean?"

"It means," he said, "that Mrs. Alessis was poisoned."

CHAPTER SEVEN

IT TOOK HER until they had once again gone outside and he had changed into civilian clothes for her to adjust to the shock. Murder was as much her territory as his, and its presence focused her mind.

"What was the poison?" she asked.

"Probably carbon tetrachloride. There aren't many that could cause this particular harm to the liver."

"You mean the cleaning agent?"

"You've heard of it?"

"It was once used by dry cleaners. There were lawsuits by families of people who died from inhaling its fumes, so it was banned."

"Exactly right," he said. "Good for you."

The compliment made her absurdly pleased. "And you really think Mrs. Alessis died from it?"

Jake took a sip of the coffee he had bought from a hallway vending machine on his way out and poured the rest on the ground. "It's a clever method. You have to be able to get close enough to give it surreptitiously. The victim doesn't die until a couple of days later. And since the compound itself can no longer be detected through toxicology tests in the body after three days, no one's really hunting a killer."

"Could this have been an accident?"

He shrugged. "Unlikely, but of course possible. We should go to her apartment to see if she has older cleaning products there containing the poison."

"You want to go *now*?"

"Absolutely. I told her family I'd want to look at the place where she died, and now there's an urgent reason. What's wrong? Are you tired?"

Strangely, she wasn't. She rejected a sarcastic answer. "Why should I be tired?"

Jake smiled at her; Manny got the feeling it was genuine. "You're a trouper," he said.

"Baby, darling, honey, sweetheart," Manny called, approaching the Porsche. She opened the door. Mycroft shied away, whimpering. "Don't be afraid. It's Mommy." She turned to Jake. "What have you done to my dog?"

He held out his hands, palms up. "Nothing. I swear."

"Then why is he acting like this?" She made kissy noises. Mycroft leaped from the car and hid under it.

"I can't imagine."

The odor of her jacket wafted up. "Oh, Jesus," she said. "I smell like death."

"Then Mycroft must be an unusual animal. Dogs usually like clothing that's been in the autopsy room."

"What? Why?"

"They think it smells like food."

"That," she said, "is the most disgusting thing I've ever heard."

"But it's true. It's not you he's scared of—"

"I should say not!" *The idea!*

"—it's somebody or something else."

They peered into the dark. Manny turned on the headlights. The bushes in front of the car were indented, as though someone had fled through them.

Theresa Alessis had lived in the basement apartment of a two-family house on a run-down street three blocks from downtown Turner. The upper floors were vacant; a sign out front said 2 APTS 4 RENT. Manny didn't imagine there'd be many takers. Even in the dark she could see that the paint was flaking and the front lawn overgrown.

"Are you sure this is okay?" she asked, as they crept their way down the uneven concrete stairs that led to Mrs. Alessis's front entrance.

"Yes. Why are you whispering?"

"Because it's three o'clock in the bloody morning."

Jake fumbled with a flowerpot outside the door and produced a key. "Right where her son said it would be."

He unlocked the door, reached in, and groped for a switch. The lights blazed on, as startling as a scream in the darkness.

The small apartment was shabby but neat. An ornate cross Manny recognized as Greek Orthodox dominated the wall over the couch, and a china cupboard contained what appeared to be a large collection of sewing thimbles.

"My grandparents were tailors," Manny said, touched. "These thimbles make me feel a certain kinship with Mrs. Alessis. Even a responsibility."

"A coincidence," Jake said. "My grandparents were tailors, too." He didn't add that, as union members, they had been beaten nearly to death because they belonged to the ILGWU.

"Maybe it's fate that we're in this together. . . . *Oh!*"

Jake came to her side. "What is it?"

Manny lifted a photograph of Theresa from a doily-covered end table. The beaming woman stood next to a young lady in a graduation gown. "It seems so odd to see her alive." She glanced at him for a reaction. "That probably sounds stupid to you."

"Not at all," he said, without irony.

"I just . . . I had such an intimate look at her, and I don't even know her. It seems wrong, somehow. And here I am, looking through her things. . . ."

"To find the reason for her death. We're investigating what looks to be a murder. If we solve it, that's the best thing we can do for her children."

Put so bluntly, it wiped away sentiment. "You're right. I don't know what I'm talking about. Sometimes I get sappy when I'm overtired." She took a deep breath. "So what are we looking for?"

"To begin with, any cleaning products containing carbon tetrachloride she might have breathed in or swallowed."

"I'll start with the bathroom."

It was right off the living room. Jake watched as she bent down to investigate the cabinet under the sink, granting him a view of an alluring tush. *Tantalizing.* There was no other word for it. He felt an unfamiliar quickening of desire. *Whoa.* She straightened. *Looks pretty good standing up, too.* He moved to the kitchen to conduct his own search.

"I've found something," she called, not masking her excitement.

"A bottle with a skull and crossbones marked DANGER: CARBON TETRACHLORIDE?"

She came into the kitchen, carrying a bottle. "This. Our Mrs. Alessis kept it hidden next to the Ajax."

Jake was accustomed to surprises and good at maintaining outward calm. But this time he gasped.

"Do you have any idea how much this stuff costs?" she asked.

He knew precisely how much. It was a fifth of Johnnie Walker Blue.

—————

"It belonged to Pete Harrigan," he told her, recalling his friend's pleasure at the gift. "Elizabeth must have told Mrs. Alessis she could have it. It's great stuff. I should know. I'm the one who gave it to him." Jake stared down at the floor.

"Yuck!"

He looked at her. She had unscrewed the top and was holding the bottle away from her.

"What's wrong?"

"This scotch has gone bad. It's rancid."

"Nonsense. Scotch is scotch. It doesn't turn the way wine does."

She handed him the bottle. He sniffed it. "Son of a bitch!" His hand trembled as he set it on the table. "You just found our poison."

Manny sat down heavily. "Good lord!" She examined the bottle. "Wait a minute. Why would anybody drink something that smelled like this?"

"Because it didn't. Theresa Alessis died yesterday. That means she drank from the bottle two or three days ago. The carbon tetrachloride has been building up in the headspace ever since. But if you opened the bottle often enough and let the gas escape, you might not notice the odor. Only about an inch is left. What she drank was enough to kill her."

He doesn't know I'm in the room, Manny realized. The look in his eyes said his brain was running at full speed, and he frowned with a concentration she had not seen before, even during the autopsy. *Handsome. Almost beautiful.*

"What are you thinking?" she asked.

He was startled into awareness of her. "I'm thinking about the color of Pete Harrigan's eyes."

CHAPTER EIGHT

Jake didn't want to waste a moment. "We've got to get to Harrigan's cottage," he said. "Grab your keys."

"But you've already been there, I thought. You were there just last week."

"Yes, to clear out the study and get rid of the furniture. This time we're looking for something different." He grabbed her wrist and started out the door.

She shook her arm free but kept up with his pace. Fatigue, excitement, bewilderment, and foreboding created a volatile cocktail in her stomach. "You think he was poisoned, don't you?"

He turned to look at her. His expression was somber. "Yes."

"But you said he was dying anyway. Why murder a dying man?"

"Don't you see?" There was exasperation in his tone. "Because of the bones."

The cottage had been broken into again. This time it had been trashed. The cardboard boxes of everyday household furnishings that Jake and Sam had packed were strewn about haphazardly.

Furniture was overturned and pillow feathers dusted the floor like snow.

They walked through the rooms, assessing the damage like residents returning home after a tornado. "How long ago do you think this happened?" Manny asked. She realized she was now holding on to his arm, but he seemed to take no notice of it.

"I spoke to Mrs. Alessis day before yesterday. She never mentioned another burglary, only that she worried about getting everything sorted and packed for the Salvation Army, said she was tired. It must've been the carbon tetrachloride affecting her."

"What do you think they were looking for, the Johnnie Walker Blue?"

"I don't know. You wouldn't have to do this much damage to figure out it isn't here."

"Maybe they trashed the place because they couldn't find it."

"More likely they were looking for something else." He stopped. "Jesus! *I* may have it. I took home a lot of stuff from the study, piled in boxes and plastic bags. I'll have to go through it as soon as I get home."

I'll help you, she thought, but felt too shy, too foreign, to say so. Instead she said, "Why do I get the feeling that you know more about this than you're letting on?"

"I don't. Really. It's one thing I learned in the ME's office: people don't change—not that often, anyway. You see someone come in dead of a knife wound, they've got half a dozen healed scars from other fights. We find old bullets in people who've died of new gunshot wounds; it's like they've been rehearsing their own ending. Why would a sophisticated killer, who's gotten away with an apparently undetectable murder, risk exposure?"

Feeling dizzy, she righted a chair and sat down. "You're scaring me. Sophisticated killer? We meet tonight to discuss a forty-year-old case of malpractice. Now you're telling me we have two murders, one of them, the housekeeper's, unintentional. And Mycroft may have been threatened. What does that mean for us? *They know we're looking!*" The last was almost a howl. The possibility of danger made her exhaustion unbearable. *Was the trip to Poughkeepsie in my lifetime?*

He put his hand on her shoulder. "All I mean," he said, "is that I don't believe someone smart and organized enough to poison Pete Harrigan with a poison as obscure as carbon tetrachloride, making it look like a natural death, would trash Pete's house." He reached for her hand. "You're exhausted. Time to go home."

At last. She started to rise. "Did you hear that?"

He stood still. "Hear what?"

"Something outside. Noises."

He dashed for the lights, extinguished them, and drew her toward the front door. "What did you hear? Be specific."

"Footsteps on the gravel? I'm not sure."

Jake cracked open the door and peered outside. In the light of the quarter moon, nothing was visible. "I don't see anything. Are you sure you really—"

She glowered at him.

"Sorry." He shut the door silently. "I'll check the back door. You stay here."

"Very funny." She followed him.

He opened the door. "I can't see anything."

She pulled out her cell phone. "I'm calling the cops." The NO SERVICE light flashed.

"No towers," he said. "In this part of the world, pristine views are more important than pristine service. Let's try Pete's phone."

It had been disconnected. "What are we supposed to do?" Manny whispered. "We can't just hide here till the sun comes up. I'm supposed to have breakfast with Patrice Perez." *Which means no sleep for me.*

He took a breath. "Then let's go." His voice was resolute.

"Fine." So was hers.

"Before we leave," he said, "I want to drop the Johnnie Walker bottle off for the sheriff. I could have left it at the scene, but I didn't want to risk it."

They started out the front. She had locked the car, yet the Porsche's door was wide open. "Oh my God!" Manny said. "Mycroft!"

She raced to the car, her heels crunching on the broken glass from her car's passenger window. Mycroft was missing. "Mycroft!" she shrieked into the darkness. "Where are you?" She turned to Jake, her eyes wide. "He's gone. Mycroft!"

"Keep it down," he urged. "They may still be around here."

She glared at him. "My dog is missing," she said sharply. "Some of us actually care about living things."

Mycroft materialized from a neighbor's yard and leaped into Manny's arms. The sobs she had suppressed for hours exploded from her throat.

Carrying her beloved as she would a newborn, she got into the car and reached for the Prada tote with his treats. "Gone," she breathed. She twisted to check the backseat. "Gone!" she screamed. "Jake!"

He was on his hands and knees, searching the ground. She rounded the car and stood over him. "Jake, my new Prada tote bag is gone!"

He looked at her, eyes blazing. "It's only a thing— calm down."

He's cracked. He's a monster. "Jake. Someone stole my *bag*. Don't you understand? It had some of my confidential legal work in it."

He rose slowly, using the door handle to help him to his feet. His pants were covered with dirt; his hair was filthy. Obviously, he had crawled under the car. *Searching for what?*

When he looked at her again, his expression had softened, and when he spoke it was with his habitual calm. "I'm sorry I snapped at you," he said. "But they took something even more important. The poisoned bottle's missing. It means whoever took it has been following us all evening and knows we know that Pete was murdered." Worry creased his forehead and made lines at the sides of his eyes. "Jesus, Manny, I'm sorry I got you into this. But we've been sucked into the vortex and there's little you or I can do about it now."

They found the Baxter County Sheriff's Office in a brick storefront just off Main Street. At 3:30 a.m. it was locked up tight, lights off. A sign on the door gave business hours as 7 a.m. to 4 p.m. and a number to dial in case of emergency. Jake flipped open his cell phone. The signal was faint but there.

He got a dispatcher who reluctantly agreed to patch him through to Sheriff Fisk's line. The sheriff was not pleased to hear from him.

"Rosen. I thought you were in New York. What's so very important you have to wake me in the middle of the night?"

Jake told him about the results of his autopsy on Theresa Alessis, his suspicion that both she and Harrigan were poisoned, the condition of Pete's cottage, the missing bottle. "It's a double murder," he finished. "I wanted to alert you as soon as possible."

"I surely am grateful," Fisk said, "but I gotta tell you: I never heard such a pile of horse manure in my life."

"You mean you don't believe me?"

"Rather than Harrigan's doctor, who already signed the death certificate: *Died of natural causes*? Not a chance."

He's an enemy, Jake realized with surprise. *Be careful.*

"Besides," Fisk went on, "you don't have a motive or a suspect.

Can you imagine the repercussions if I halt the mall project again because of some city doctor's cockamamy theory? Maybe there was a bottle of scotch, maybe there wasn't. Maybe Harrigan killed himself because he didn't want to live through the pain of the cancer. Sickness can screw up your head. He probably never thought about the maid. Maybe you put poison in the bottle before you gave it to him—for certain you'd be my first suspect. And maybe we'll say good night nice and polite, and you and your lady friend can get back to the city and not bother us again." The receiver slammed down.

He was just as defensive about the bones, Jake thought. I wonder if he gets a kickback on the mall deal? He told Manny about his conversation as they got in the car. "He's right about the hard evidence," Jake said. "There's no proof anybody was murdered." He stretched. "You sure you're okay to drive?"

"Unless you've learned to use a stick in the past eight hours, what choice do I have?" She started the car. She was so tired she envied his shabby loafers.

They drove in silence for a while. Jake dozed against the window, a contented Mycroft curled on his lap. His eyelids are twitching, she noticed. I'll bet he saws people in half when he sleeps. She wanted to touch him, to ease his tension and her own. She wanted to feel the warmth of his hand on her face. She wanted to—

"Manny!" He sat bolt upright.

"What's the matter?"

"Fisk told *both of us* to get back to the city. But I never mentioned you. How the hell did he know you were with me?"

CHAPTER NINE

JAKE STOPPED at his apartment only long enough to shower and change clothes before heading to his office next to Bellevue Hospital, his mind not tired even if his body was. *Was Fisk the man who had followed them, terrified Mycroft, and stolen the Johnnie Walker bottle? Did he know who the murderer was? Was he the murderer himself?* A murder investigation would halt construction of the mall, even if the unidentified bones didn't. *Did Fisk have a financial interest in the mall? Did Mayor Stevenson? Was there a conspiracy with Reynolds Construction to bilk Baxter County and the State of New York out of millions?*

These were the questions that obsessed him, and he found it difficult to concentrate on the paperwork that lay before him. *How much time can I afford to give to the case when my duty is to this ME's office? What responsibility do I have to solve it? Would I involve Manny again? If not, should I ask her to go out with me?*

He shook his head to clear it—*What in God's name are you thinking about?*—and decided his allegiance was to Pete Harrigan. *Long as it takes. Don't let his murderer go free.*

A knock on the door brought his mind back to his office. "Come in, Wally."

Dr. Walter Winnick always knocked, though Jake had told him a hundred times he didn't have to; the office was as much his as Jake's. The man was excessively shy, probably because of his club-foot, but his education was superb—Harrigan, after all, had been his mentor at Columbia. Wally had taken Pete's death hard, and he took over much of Jake's paperwork uncomplainingly. The two often ate lunch together, usually at a cheap health-food restaurant close to the office that Wally liked more than Jake did. Their talk avoided the personal, though Jake knew that Wally had worked for years near Santa Fe, New Mexico, in a school for autistic and schizophrenic children: an ideal place, Jake thought, for a man uncomfortable in normal society. Still, Wally had matured enough to survive in the city, and Jake had been happy to hire him on Pete's recommendation. When he once asked Wally if he could look at his foot in the hope of finding some treatment, Wally had bridled like a wild horse under a saddle. Actually, once a man reached Wally's age—about forty, Jake guessed, though he seemed much younger—there was little one *could* do. Clubfoot is a con-genital condition. The tendons in the foot and ankle are too short at birth to produce a normal foot, and the best time for surgery is when the patient is still an infant. Jake never learned why Wally's parents had not opted for surgery, but then again, the sixties were another time. Jake never brought up the subject again.

Wally lived in a tiny apartment (Jake had visited once; his impression was of wall-to-wall books and mutual unease), liked Harrison Ford movies and medical thrillers, and dated a girl built like a minaret who occasionally picked Wally up at the office. Wally always seemed happy for what he had, not angry about what he didn't have.

"Reporting for duty," Wally said, as he had every morning in the three years he'd worked for Jake. He was wearing his signature blue button-down shirt under his white coat. Early on, Jake had wondered if he owned any other kind. The answer seemed to be no. "What's on the agenda?"

"How would you like some fresh air?"

"A vacation? Dr. Rosen, you know I never—"

"I'm not suggesting one. I need someone to do a little snooping for me upstate."

"Snooping. Sounds great." His slow, careful gait brought him to Jake's desk. "Details?"

"There's a mall being built in a town called Turner in Baxter County."

"Where Dr. Harrigan lived! I've visited him there."

"Then you know it. Good. I think the mall's a boondoggle, a scam to enrich town officials at citizens' expense. The developer is R. Seward Reynolds, out of Albany, and if my guess is right, there's a payoff coming to the sheriff—his name's Fisk—and maybe to Mayor Stevenson and to a woman named Crespy who runs the historical society." He paused. Wally's homely face was staring at him with the intensity of an acolyte.

"Anyway," Jake went on, "at least for the moment, my interest is in Fisk, not the others. I want you go up there, study the public records, see what you can find. Competitive bids if any, kickbacks, the sheriff's handprints on a project he has no business being linked to. That sort of thing."

Wally was taking notes. "This is outside an ME's usual jurisdiction," he said. "Does it have anything to do with Dr. Harrigan?"

"Only indirectly." Jake had decided to tell Wally nothing about his suspicions. He didn't want to upset his assistant before he was sure. "When I saw him last, Pete told me he was positive there was fraud going on, and it really rankled. I told him I'd look into it." He smiled. "You are my eyes and ears."

Wally blushed. "One more question: How does a man with a clubfoot go about snooping inconspicuously?"

The question troubled Jake; he had thought about it. "Make up an excuse for your being there. A research paper on the area. A study of mental hospitals. Whatever. If there's a hint of trouble, beat it back here."

Wally stood. "When do I leave?"

Jake looked at his watch. "How about half an hour ago?"

It was nearly six o'clock in the morning when Manny finally pulled her Murphy bed out of the wall. Fully clothed, she lay down on top of her rose silk quilt to take a nap before she washed and dried her hair. For the first time, she appreciated the cocoonlike nature of her tiny studio. It felt protective. The tops of her white beech modular units were stacked with shoe boxes, *lots* of shoe boxes. Her kitchen—a perfect size for take-out containers—was behind a shoji screen. Manny had decided to live in the best building on Central Park South. The outside world, her adversaries, would see success in her address. And she would feel successful every time she walked through the lobby.

The rest of the apartment was impeccably decorated. "No matter how small the project, do it right," her mother had told her. Her fax, printer, notebook, and flat-screen TV, in a neat row on the marble table across from her bed, composed her working area. Framed historical legal documents dotted the walls above the contemporary Italian-design sofa.

Still, nothing made her comfortable now; visions of Mrs. Alessis filled her head. At last, with Mycroft cuddled tightly in her arms, she drifted off.

After two hours of haunted sleep, Manny leaped out of bed. Eight o'clock. No time for her hair; she had to walk Mycroft. She threw on her black Donna Karan microfiber dress and matching black boots with rubber soles so she could sprint the four blocks to her breakfast appointment. She was cold when she went outside with Mycroft, so back at her apartment she put on her black TSE cashmere swing coat and at the last moment, for color, added a hunter-green Etro fox-fur collar. *To look at me you'd never know I spent last night with a corpse.*

She reached Le Parker Meridien hotel only ten minutes late. A woman who had to be Patrice Lyons Perez was waiting in the lobby. *Oops. Wrong clothes. I should have dressed appropriately.*

She had wanted to cheer her new client by taking her to a fancy breakfast at the Meridien, but now that she saw her perched on the edge of a squarish modern chair, she realized she hadn't done her a favor. Hollow-eyed and gaunt, clad in a long yellow polyester dress covered with pink roses, she seemed miserable and out of place. An old blue parka lay on the arm of the chair, and she looked around the lobby as though wanting to flee.

Manny put on a smile and extended her hand. "Patrice. I'm Philomena Manfreda. It's nice to meet you in person."

Patrice stood. The small hand she put in Manny's was limp and soft. *Like Play-Doh.*

"Hi," she said.

"Thanks for coming all this way. I'm so sorry I'm late. Did you have any trouble getting to midtown from Queens?"

"Actually, I'm not staying with my mom's cousin. I'm staying here."

Good grief. Does she know how much it costs? "At the Meridien?"

"Dr. Rosen fixed it up for me after I told him where we were meeting for breakfast. He paid for the room in advance."

Patrice's teeth were bad, but her smile was so genuine and childlike it made Manny catch her breath.

"He took care of everything," Patrice continued.

"Nice of him," Manny said. *And not surprising. The man has his good qualities as well as his faults.*

"He's a wonderful man."

I wouldn't go that far. "Are you hungry?"

"Very. All I had for dinner was a slice of pizza. It was the only thing I could find in this neighborhood that seemed . . . affordable. And it was still expensive, at least compared to home."

"You should've ordered room service."

"Oh, no," Patrice said gravely. "That wouldn't be right. I'm not a freeloader, Ms. Manfreda."

She followed Manny around the corner to a place that was classically Manhattan: counter stools, a pressed-tin ceiling, immigrant Greek owners. But the ambiance seemed lost on Patrice, who ordered a poached egg, plain white toast, and tea.

Manny had coffee. It was all she had ingested since dinner, and all she wanted. The smell of formaldehyde still lingered in her head.

Patrice retrieved a worn manila envelope from her bag and laid it down carefully, making sure the table was clear of spills. "I didn't want to put these in the mail. They're letters from my dad. I told Dr. Rosen about them, and he thought they might help."

There's an appealing eagerness here. Manny was beginning to like her. "When your father was at Turner, did he ever call you? Was he allowed to do that?"

"A few times," she said, "but not very often. Not at all in the couple of months before he stopped writing."

"When he did call, did he ever mention anything about friends he might've had there? People he spent time with?"

"He told me stories sometimes, fun stuff about people going on vacations. But I think he made most of it up."

"Do you remember anything about a girl in her late teens or early twenties?"

Patrice bowed her head. "That's why Mom died heartbroken. She believed he'd run off with another woman." She sat up straighter. "But I don't."

Manny leaned forward. "Patrice, there were other skeletons found with your father's. Two were men. One was female, a young female."

She seems angry now. Why? "I want to find out about my father. I loved him and my mother. But he hurt us when he left." She turned her wrists upward, displaying healed, thin parallel scars. *A suicide attempt. Maybe more than one.* "And I hurt Mom when I ran away from home. . . ." She paused, evidently reliving the past. "Dr. Rosen said that since four bodies were found, maybe it was an old graveyard."

"He doesn't really think so. The bodies weren't properly buried, just put in the ground. It's one of the facts that makes us wonder if the four were mistreated."

"What do their families say?"

"We don't know. The other remains haven't been identified yet."

"How awful!" *Please don't cry.* "Do you think somebody will find out who they are?"

"Dr. Rosen's working on it. In the meantime, I'll try to make sure that no remains are disposed of until they're identified. The remains may be vital to our case, and I want to make sure to preserve them. Oh, and don't worry about the cost. I won't ask you to pay for anything unless we get a monetary award, in which case my firm gets one-third."

Patrice squinted at her. *Anger again, more overt.* "I *knew* it," she said. "I knew somebody like you wouldn't just *help* me. I'm not after money. I just want to find out what happened to my dad."

"I know. And I sympathize. But if we find out he was mistreated in the hospital, wouldn't you want to make whoever's responsible pay?"

She thought about it. "If somebody did something really wrong, could he still go to jail? That'd be the way to make him pay, not by getting money from him."

"Maybe. But after all this time, criminal behavior would be hard to prove, and the perpetrator might be dead. The only way to get satisfaction is to sue the government. It doesn't mean you're greedy. It just means you want to hold the system accountable. And maybe it'll keep another family from suffering the way you have. Your father was a hero; he fought for his country. The circumstances of his death are important. I want both for you to have the truth and for the person who did this to be punished. The way to get at that person, dead or alive, is through a lawsuit. But I won't mislead you. It's going to be a tough fight."

It was a speech Manny had given many times before, and it had the virtue of being true. Justice, immediate or long delayed, had to be fought for, particularly if the victim was unable to fight for herself. The part of the settlement she received in Patrice's case, assuming she won, would pay for the losing fights and broken hearts, including her own.

She watched relief flow into Patrice's face. *I've gotten through.*

"Do you remember your father ever telling you he was being treated with electroshock therapy?"

Patrice gasped. "No. Is that what killed him?"

"Might have. Dr. Rosen says it's a possibility."

"He died during his treatment? And they put him in the ground so nobody would know they'd screwed up?"

Healthy anger now. We're allies. "I don't know," Manny said, squeezing Patrice's hand. "But together we're going to find out."

CHAPTER TEN

KENNETH BOYD was standing on the sidewalk in front of Manny's office when she drove up. Dressed in his black velveteen jacket with a fuchsia and orange brocade silk lining, he looked ready to escort her to the opera rather than a day in court.

He slid into the passenger seat of the Porsche. "*Who* was sitting in this seat, or perhaps I should ask *what* you were doing in it? With this much legroom, you either had a date with a basketball player or you—"

Manny laughed. "Stop right there. Actually, the seat was occupied by Dr. Rosen."

"*The* Dr. Rosen? The traitorous, lying, moneygrubbing, amoral son of a bitch?"

"The very one. Do you want to know what I was up to?"

"Of course I do, girlfriend! Spit it out. That is, if it's suitable for my delicate ears."

"I was with a naked body."

"I knew it! Shocking, but about time."

"A *dead* naked body. I assisted Dr. Rigor Mortis, as you call him, at an autopsy. I was with him when he sliced open—"

"No more!" Kenneth shouted. "Unsuitable!" He stared at her. "You gotta be careful who you consort with. I know you watch out for me, but remember, I watch out for you, too." He handed her the papers he had prepared for her. "The petition."

She glanced through it. "You're a godsend. There isn't another paralegal who could have drafted this so quickly."

"I can be buttered up day or night. But a petition to stop the state from burying bones? That message you left for me before you met with Perez was wacko, even for you."

"Not really. The Baxter County judge agreed to hear my application to preserve the skeletons on an emergency basis. I called the lawyer for Baxter County and community hospital to tell him what I'm doing, and he'll be in court, kicking and screaming, to try to stop me." She started the car. "By the way, you'll have to get the passenger window replaced. I'll fill you in as we drive up to Turner."

The old mahogany walls of the once-proud courtroom were patched with mismatched walnut pasteboard. *The common man gets pasteboard, the rich corporation marble.* Even worse, the client had to pay a filing fee before being permitted to seek justice. She had laid out the money, knowing her chances of ever seeing it again were slim to nonexistent.

She knew the attorney going up against her: good ol' fat toupeed Chester Gruen, a member of the old boys' club, whom she had met at her first Bar Association meeting in New York. There he had charmed her by pointing to his crotch. "You'll never be a match for *this* in the courtroom," he had said. Manny had squinted. "I'm sorry. I seem to have forgotten my magnifying glass." He'll remember me, she thought now, fidgeting as they waited at counsel tables for the judge to take the bench.

"What are you so impatient about, Ms. Manfreda? Your client ain't going anyplace," Gruen said, roaring at his own witticism.

Manny stifled the temptation to ask if *it* had gotten any bigger since she'd last seen him. Probably not, she decided, and comforted herself with the notion that it had shrunk.

Judge Melvin Bradford III, it turned out, was as fidgety as she. Manny made her case succinctly, stressing the need to identify all the people who had been buried with Lyons in case there was a connection between them that could add to her contention that Turner Psychiatric had been remiss, at the very least.

Gruen, who represented both Baxter County and its hospital— a blatant conflict of interest, Manny told herself—tried to dismiss the suit as frivolous and a nuisance, "designed to cost the county taxpayers their hard-earned pay in these economically troubled times" and to "smear with false charges an institution that was the pride of Turner Township for more than a century."

He hadn't done his homework; thanks to Kenneth, Manny had. Judge Bradford, who had evidently listened to Gruen too many times, allowed her the first order ever granted in the State of New York to preserve four skeletons, dirt, the results of toxicological testing, X-rays if any, autopsy reports, medical examiner's notes and files, photos, police officers' reports and notes, clothing, medical records, paraffin blocks, formal-fixed tissues, microscopic slides, "and a whole lot of other stuff—anything you need."

Euphoric, Manny skipped out of the courtroom, ignoring Gruen, who had approached the bench to ask for a meeting in judge's chambers.

"That was fast," Kenneth said. "After we serve the order on the hospital, we'll be home by supper."

"I don't think so. As long as we're here and finished so early, I thought we might take a little side trip on Patrice's behalf. See if I can rouse some ghosts."

———

It took Jake three hours to complete his morning autopsies, and he still hadn't started on the paperwork. Pederson'll ream me a new one if I don't get it done, he thought, though the words swam before his eyes. Under Harrigan, Pederson's predecessor, there were far fewer forms with far fewer necessary signatures, and a doctor could get home at a decent hour. He had about decided that rest was worth a tongue-lashing when the phone rang.

"Dr. Rosen?" A man's voice, oozing honey. Bad news.

"Speaking."

"My firm represents R. Seward Reynolds, the developer of the Turner Mall."

"And your name is . . . ?"

"Michael Thompson of Javalovich, Custer, Thompson and Warbler. We understand that your representative is in Baxter County trying to preserve the skeletons and close up the area where they were found, and that you yourself have been espousing preposterous theories that could cause our client financial harm."

Manny's work. Good girl! And wouldn't she love it if she knew he called her my "representative." "Who told you that?"

"We don't reveal client confidences. We simply wanted to tell you, as a courtesy, that our client is prepared to litigate for any monies lost as a result of your or your representative's actions. To put it plainly: Stick to your own job."

Jake usually responded with great cool, but he had a few trigger points. Threats were high on his short list. Anger flooded his bloodstream like a serum. "Mr. Thompson, are you threatening me? You tell your client that if he tries to stop me or my representative, I'll bury *his* bones next to those of Mr. Lyons and personally build a shopping center over them." He slammed down the phone, surprised at the vehemence of his loathing.

The phone rang again.

"Look, you, if you ever—"

"Dr. Rosen," said a woman's breathless voice, "thank God you're there! You've got to help us. Something awful's happened."

Jake rubbed at the vein throbbing in his temple. "Who is this?"

"It's Paula Koros, Theresa Alessis's daughter."

His breathing slowed. "Of course Ms. Koros. Forgive me for shouting. I was just about to call you. I've completed the autopsy of your mother's body." *How best to break it to her?*

She didn't give him a chance. "I'm at the funeral home. The whole family's here. Dr. Rosen, the body in the coffin—it's not my mother. It's a different woman altogether."

He knew the body he'd worked on was Mrs. Alessis; he had seen her alive a few days before. But there were two other bodies at the morgue. Was it possible . . . ?

He called Baxter Community Hospital and got the morgue attendant, a man who sounded not much older than eighteen.

"Last night I performed an autopsy on a woman named Theresa Alessis. She was to be transported this morning to the Fairview Funeral Home, only the wrong body went to that funeral parlor. I need to know what other female bodies were in the morgue last night."

"I'm not sure I'm authorized to give out that information."

"This is urgent! Tell me *now*!" Jake ordered.

The answer came back quickly. "There were two other bodies in the morgue: one female, one male. Female was Brigit Reilly, seventy-five. Husband deceased. No children. The death certificate says Alzheimer's. File says she lived at Sweetbrook."

"A nursing home."

"Yes, sir."

"And where was Mrs. Reilly's body sent for preparation?"

"Shady Briar. It's like forty minutes away. Only it's kinda weird." He paused.

Jake sighed in frustration. "What's weird?"

"The van for the county cemetery came here late this morning, looking for Mrs. Reilly. I told them she was gone, that we had received instructions to send her to Shady Briar for private internment."

The throbbing grew worse. "Mrs. Reilly was initially supposed to be buried in a pauper's grave?"

"Yes, sir."

"Only the body now seems to be at a third place, Fairview?"

"Seems so." Jake could visualize the shrug.

The mix-up was too coincidental. It felt ominous to Jake. Pete's murder. The stolen bottle. Thompson's call about the bones. The trashing of Pete's house. And now a missing body. "Let me have the numbers for Sweetbrook and Shady Briar. I tell you, young man, if this is a hospital error . . ." *But it isn't. It's something more.*

At Sweetbrook, a nurse from the Alzheimer's wing agreed to go to the Fairview Funeral Home to look at the body and to call Jake on his pager once she had. An hour later, his suspicion was verified: The body that lay before Theresa Alessis's grieving family was, in fact, Brigit Reilly.

He called Shady Briar. "My name is Dr. Jake Rosen and I'm trying to locate a body that was delivered to your funeral home this morning," he told the director.

"We're not strictly a funeral home," the man said. "We're a mausoleum, for the interment of remains. As well as a crematorium, of course."

A curlicue of dread snaked toward his heart. "The body is cremated?"

"Indeed. At the request of her son."

"She didn't have any children! That wasn't Mrs. Reilly. Mrs. Reilly is lying in a casket at the Fairview Funeral Home in Turner."

"Impossible," the director said. "You're mistaken, Dr. Rosen. We received instructions from Mrs. Reilly's son early this morning; my service rang me around six. He told me his mother had expired at Baxter Community Hospital and he wanted her cremated as soon as possible. We picked her up—her name was clearly present on the tag on the body bag. I met him myself. A polite man. Very clean. He paid for our services in cash. And we honor our commitments, doctor."

The dread struck. He felt dizzy. "What did the son look like?"

"Hard to say. I'm not good at describing people when they're perpendicular." He chuckled. "Average build, brown hair, in his forties."

"Did he mention picking up the ashes or make any arrangements for a remains mausoleum?"

"Not as of now."

"Isn't that unusual?"

"Not at all. Remains sometimes go unclaimed for years, regardless of the original intention. People don't know what to do with them. That's why we offer eternal storage in our peaceful—"

"Hold on to those ashes. Don't release them to anyone unless you personally deliver them to the Alessis family at Fairview."

"The Alessis family? Whatever for?"

"I don't think you heard me. You cremated the wrong woman. That 'son' hired you to get rid of evidence."

A beat. "Evidence?"

"Mrs. Alessis was murdered."

"Heavenly God!"

"God," said Jake, "had nothing to do with it."

Edward Dyson, the administrator of Baxter Community Hospital, was smarm incarnate. "You didn't have to bring the papers personally," he told Manny in his office. "Judge Bradford called me himself. Too late, though," he said as he gnawed on a jelly bean from the jar on his desk.

The breath went out of her; she felt she'd been punched in the chest. "Too late?"

Instead of answering, Dyson pressed a button by his phone. In moments, a thin man, appearing only old enough to have just graduated high school, arrived at the office door. "Tommy," the administrator said, "this is Ms. Manfreda. Tell her what you told me."

"Mr. Dyson said we gotta hang on to those skeletons from the mental bin. But I told him they already got sent away."

Manny stood. "When?"

"This morning." He cowered like a frightened puppy. "Don't tell me I did another thing wrong. First I release bodies to the wrong funeral homes, and now bones are missing."

Calm down. Deep breath. "You were on duty when the four skeletons were released?"

"Yes, ma'am."

"I need to know about the man who picked them up."

"Wasn't no man. It was a lady." He sounded victorious, as though he'd won a game of gin rummy.

"Okay, a lady. Describe her."

"Old."

"How old?"

"Fortyish." Manny chuckled to herself. "Don't know what color hair. Wore a scarf." His brow creased in concentration. "Wore one of those shapeless dresses, sounds like a cow."

"A muumuu?"

"That's it. I didn't pay much attention to her. She had the release papers with her."

Dyson proffered a few sheets of bright yellow paper. "This was a proper transfer," he said. "Look. Tommy did just right."

Manny glanced at the first page. "The bones were transferred to the New York City morgue? And the X-rays? And the files? Care of *Dr. Jacob Rosen?*"

"Yup. The woman said she was from his office. Dr. Rosen himself called me later around noon, but it was about something different. About a body, not bones. Doc Harrigan had the bones laid out in the drawers. I put them in body bags and gave them to the lady."

Manny felt a wash of relief, pissed as she was that Jake hadn't told her. The New York City morgue was probably the safest place in the world for the bones to be. *I'll call him. Give him a hard time about wasted effort. He can tell me about the body. Maybe we should meet, discuss the advantages of teamwork.* She smiled to herself. *That would be nice.*

She turned to Dyson. "Can I have a photocopy of this release?"

He barely glanced at her. "Of course. My secretary will make one for you on your way out."

Jake had just gotten off the phone with Paula Koros, who took the news about her mother's body with a defeated resignation that would, he guessed, later turn to rage. A new client for Manny, he thought.

His phone rang: the lawyer herself. "Want to hear the Italian word for jackass?" she asked.

"Not particularly. In what context?"

"In the context that Kenneth and I killed ourselves to convince a judge to preserve the Turner skeletons. Mission accomplished. Why didn't you *tell* me you were transferring them to New York?"

He felt a stab of pain in his eyes. "I wasn't."

"I'm talking Skeletons One, Two, Three, and Four and all the other 'stuff,' to use Judge Bradford's elegant terminology."

"I didn't have them transferred." He heard her gasp.

"You must have. I'm holding a transfer order with your signature on it."

"It can't be my signature because I never signed a transfer. Whoever authorized those remains to be picked up, it wasn't me. And the bones aren't in the city morgue, that I can guarantee you."

Despair engulfed her. Without the bones, she couldn't use them as evidence against whoever killed Harrigan and Mrs. Alessis, help Patrice, team up with Jake. She felt empty, drained of spirit, spent.

"We're being outthought, outmaneuvered," she said.

"There's more to it than that," he agreed. "The bones and the poison are part of a single puzzle. We're up against someone who'll kill to keep it from being put together."

CHAPTER ELEVEN

THERE WAS ONE more place to look. Slowly, methodically, Manny drove with Kenneth to the Turner Psychiatric Institute.

They arrived at five o'clock. She insisted that Kenneth wait in the Porsche. She'd need him as a getaway driver, she said, if she had to leave in a hurry—she was, after all, planning on breaking and entering. She reached into the glove compartment for a flashlight.

"But the hospital's defunct," Kenneth said. "Died like its patients. You won't find anything here."

"There may still be records, stuff that was overlooked. We've lost all the evidence, Kenneth. If I don't find anything, this *case* is defunct."

He settled back in the seat. "This may be a bad way of putting it, sister. But it's your funeral."

Now Manny stood before a huge dilapidated gray building that stood at the crest of a hill like a medieval castle. Its lights were out, its door locked. She'd studied the architectural plans and knew this was Serenity Hall, once the hospital's only structure, with offices on the ground floor and patients' rooms above. Manny counted six stories. She noted that the windows on the higher floors were exceedingly narrow, probably so that suicidal patients couldn't hurl themselves out. ADMINISTRATION read a sign on the front door. *This must be where they kept their files, even when the hospital expanded. If they wanted to hide a file, not send it to Poughkeepsie, it'd still be here.* She tried the door. Locked. A side door was also locked, as was another at the back. The windows were shut, and when she peered through the filthy panes, she saw they fronted wire mesh; she'd have to break the glass and cut the wires if she wanted to get inside.

She was suddenly struck by the futility of her task. *Break in and search through six floors and a basement? Are you out of your mind?*

She stepped back. They had driven up a steep road to get to the virtually deserted parking lot by the entrance; in the distance she could see the field in which the bones had been found. The sun was low in the sky, casting shadows of outlying buildings across grass that seemed almost black, and the air was rapidly growing colder. *Maybe there's somebody somewhere.* She could make out a light down the hill, and though she had no idea whether the building was even on the hospital grounds, she started for it. Another building, completely dark, loomed to her right, appearing suddenly in the gloom as though it had just arrived. Startled, Manny approached it. A barely legible sign over the door read PROMISE HOUSE. She recognized the name. When Turner Psychiatric was in operation, this was the residence of patients who needed the least care. It too was locked. She rubbed a hole in the coating of grime on a corner window, shone her flashlight, and was rewarded with a view of a rusty bed frame tipped over onto a mattress covered in green mold, walls stained with water damage, the shredded pages of old magazines, and the body of a dead rat. The promise had been broken.

Jesus God! A squirrel dashed between her legs, raising gooseflesh on every part of her body. She let out a yelp, then stifled it, not wanting to be discovered. *Some sign of human life would be nice, though.* Gathering clouds and a chill wind promised rain.

To her left stood a brick building, the front of which was a glass sunroom. Most of the panes had been smashed; inside was a shambles of rocks, bricks, broken beer bottles, glass shards, dead pigeons. The dining hall, Manny knew; patients would eat in the sunlight in summer. She began to see the facility as she had seen it in photographs of its heyday: an elegant manicured home to women with "nervous conditions" and men with drinking problems who could afford the prices. In later years it had faced the same obstacles as any large mental institution: inadequate staff, patients drugged out of their gourds, only enough money to feed them gruel and Jell-O. *There's something terrible about a place that used to house so many people, even crazy people, broken down like this. It feels wrong, like a summer camp in winter. Or like a prison.* She felt a wave of pity for Lieutenant James A. Lyons.

She moved on, though she realized the light she was heading for was still too far away to be part of the property. A little farther down the path was a small squat building, maybe eight feet long and ten feet high, its one small window almost at the top. With a stab of anguish, Manny knew what it was: the Seclusion Room, where the most troubled patients were sent. "It is a spiritual sanctuary," a brochure for the Turner Mental Hospital had proclaimed, "a place where the troubled can regain peace." *Bullshit,* had been Manny's reaction when she'd read that, and *bullshit* was her reaction now. It was a confinement cell, not a sanctuary. If you wanted to use it to discipline a patient or break his will, you could do it here, away from the attention of other patients and nonessential staff.

Manny tried the door. It opened. Like a spelunker, she aimed her flashlight at the interior. Padded walls, she realized with a shiver. The room contained a cot and tattered mattress, a sink, and a toilet; nothing else. Although she knew there were no records to be found here, she stepped inside, her mind alive with fantasies born of a dozen horror movies. By now it was almost pitch-dark outside; her flashlight provided the only illumination.

On the left wall, a portion of the padding had been torn aside, revealing a white stucco wall, scribbled over with dark ink. Writing? *Yes!* Manny bent to investigate. The hole was at the level of her waist. The writing on the stucco might have been a child's, or a grown person's writing from his knees. She got on her knees and concentrated the light on the writing. The message sprang into clarity:

Please, God, deliver me. End my suffering.
Have mercy on my soul.

                          I d la S

Manny could hear the sound of her own heart beating as she stood up. *Poor tortured creature. What did they do to you?*

Warm air touched the back of her neck, and for a moment she couldn't identify its source. When she did, it was with a terror so great she knew what she was experiencing now would haunt her forever. *Breath. Rhythmic breathing. Human. Somebody's standing behind me.*

Her own breath died in her chest. She wheeled around, the flashlight making kaleidoscopic designs on the padding. "Who are you?" But there was nothing in the room except the meager furniture and the white padding to protect the insane. The open door testified to the route the intruder had taken.

There was someone here. I know it. Too shaken to scream, but not to run, Manny raced out of the Seclusion Room, up the hill past Promise House and Serenity Hall, and into the security of Kenneth's waxed arms and the glorious smell of safety.

CHAPTER TWELVE

SHE CALLED JAKE and told him what had happened. He was still in his office.

"Where are you?" he asked.

"My apartment. Kenneth drove me."

"Is he with you?"

"I sent him home."

"Then I'll come over."

She was tempted. "Why?"

"I don't want you staying alone. You're in shock. The reaction might be bad when you come out of it."

"I'm over the shock. Really. I was scared. Now I'm more than scared. I'm pissed off and really angry."

"At least come to my office first thing tomorrow."

"Why?"

"I want you to tell me everything again. See if you left out anything." He paused. "And I want to see you. Make sure you're all right."

Kindness. Warmth filled her like helium. "Say that last part again."

"I want to make sure you're all right."

"No. Just before that."

"I want to see you."
Yes.

She checked the locks, drew a bath, checked the locks again, and wallowed in warm water until the tension in her body eased and she was able to breathe normally. Dressed in a cashmere sweat suit—she realized with astonishment that she didn't care how she looked—she took Mycroft for a walk, came home, fed him, and, not hungry herself, went to bed.

The phone rang. *Don't bother.* It kept ringing. "All right," she grumbled, and picked up the receiver.

"I've decided not to go any further." A mumbled voice. Patrice.

"What did you say?"

"I'm not going any further with this, Ms. Manfreda. I've given it some more thought, and I don't want to go ahead."

Who got to her? "What are you talking about? We've taken the first step, got the court to sign the order keeping the skeletons." *All right, so we lost the bones. We'll find them again.* "We're on the way to finding out about your father's death, after all these years."

"I'm sorry. I—"

"At least let me come to New Jersey and see you and your daughter."

"That's just it. My daughter's going to make something out of her life. She's at the top of her class. I can't risk anything interfering with that."

"Why would investigating your father's death bring any harm to your daughter?"

Patrice was silent.

She's scared. "Has something happened? You've got to tell me."

A whisper. "You shouldn't have gone back to Turner."

My God! "How do you know I went there?"

A pause. Then: "I don't want to talk about it."

"You have to. This is important—for your father."

"My father's been dead to me for forty years. My daughter's alive now. I intend to keep it that way. Let his past stay buried with him."

"Someone's threatened you, haven't they?"

Silence.

"I can hire a private investigator to protect her, protect you, until we get the police—"

"No police! When the man calls again, I'll tell him I'm through. I'm finished with you and my father. I thank you, Ms. Manfreda, but please don't try to contact me again."

Jake slept on the couch in his office, waking up periodically with thoughts of Manny—that there was no call from her was either good or bad news, good if she was resting comfortably, bad if she was still frightened but didn't want to disturb him. Or if something else had happened to her, a thought he pushed away immediately by thinking of Pete.

What was so important that people generations apart would kill for today? The four skeletons were missing. What would they tell him if they were found? Even without her whole body, Jake still had Mrs. Alessis's liver samples, proof she had been poisoned. Now he needed scientific proof that Pete had been murdered—the kind that would convince a prosecutor to take the case.

In the morning, he called Elizabeth on her cell phone. It was something he dreaded—the worst, in a career that necessitated tough calls.

"It's Jake."

"Jake! I never thanked you for picking up my dad's things."

"I'm sorry the place was ransacked after I was finished."

"So you heard about that."

"Yes."

"And about Mrs. Alessis?"

"Actually, I was up there a few nights ago. Her daughter asked me to do her autopsy." He took a breath. *Now or never.* "Which brings me to why I'm calling."

Ice on her end of the line. "Oh?"

"The autopsy showed Mrs. Alessis was poisoned. It turns out the poison was in a bottle of whiskey I took to your father that we shared the last night I was with him. Obviously, the poison was added after I left. I found the bottle in Mrs. Alessis's apartment. It had carbon tetrachloride in it, which showed up in Mrs. Alessis's liver. She may or may not have been the intended victim."

Jake waited for Elizabeth to realize the implications. "Go on," she finally said.

Spell it out. "I think the poison was meant for your father. The only way to know for sure is to exhume the body and look for the very specific damage to the liver this poison would cause."

"Noooo!" It was more a wail than a word.

"Elizabeth, please. I need to find out."

He could hear her fight for control. "You mean you want to dig him up and cut him into pieces?"

"You know it's not like that. It's science. Science your father pioneered."

"I'm sorry. It's *exactly* like that. When I was twelve, Dad took me to an autopsy. He thought I was old enough to handle it. He was wrong. Everlastingly wrong. I still have nightmares. And the thought of you doing that to my father—"

"Look at it from his point of view. The death certificate says he died of natural causes. I don't think he did. Pete was a scientist. He'd want us to know the truth."

"I don't know his point of view. I only know mine and Daniel's. He thinks the autopsy process is barbaric."

"Hear me out. If he was murdered, don't you want whoever did it to be punished? Doesn't he deserve justice?"

"What if it turns out he poisoned himself? I don't want to know that. Suicide's a sin against God. Besides, I have enough justice to deal with here in my job. Please, Jake. Dad's buried. He died of cancer. Let it be."

Manny didn't see it that way. She came to Jake's office around eight, looking haggard—*and beautiful.* His impulse was to put his arms around her, but instead he just listened as she went through the events at Turner.

"I want you off the case," he said when she'd finished.

"And you'll carry on alone?"

"Until I get enough to call in the police."

"*Enough* as in 'I don't have the bones, I don't have Mrs. A's body, Pete is six feet under, and if I keep investigating I'll probably be killed'?"

He laughed. "That's about it."

"Well, with all that good stuff going for you, I stay on the case." She saw indecision in his eyes. "We once compared lists of things we hate. Threats and intimidation have just taken first and second place on mine. I've seen you look at me—you think I am a frail and helpless female. That is so male. But I'm a monster when I'm mad, and whoever it was who breathed on me last night has gotten me *pissed off.* We work together. That's final."

Now he did hug her. Got up, walked around the desk, stood by her side, and hugged her. His heart, he realized, was dancing.

Back behind his desk, he told her about his conversation with Elizabeth.

And then, because Manny simply *had* to do some of her own work, they agreed to meet the next night at Jake's house.

CHAPTER THIRTEEN

It was an unseasonably cold morning in Queens. Like so many other things that belonged to the city, the heater in Jake's official car wasn't working, and he stood at the gravesite, wishing the sun would rise faster. Armed with the exhumation order, Jake had awakened the cemetery director at midnight to fax a copy to him and arrange for a 6 a.m. start.

He was dressed in jeans, old sneakers, a polo shirt, and a light jacket, inadequate insulation for a chilly morning but perfect for a dig.

He looked at his watch: 6:32. The grounds crew hadn't arrived yet.

At this hour, the cemetery was peaceful—even, he had to admit, beautiful. The rising sun glinted off the stained-glass windows of the mausoleums, elaborate monuments to the wealthy and powerful of a bygone era, painting the simpler stones with fantastic hues. The cemetery, he knew, had plots dating back to the late eighteenth century. It had expanded in every direction, not slowing down until the 1990s when the Catholic Church had begun to allow cremation. When Jake had started at the ME's office, almost all bodies were buried; now nearly a third were reduced to ashes.

Jake had just taken out his cell phone to call the grounds crew when he heard them coming. It had been only a week since Pete's burial, so their job would be simple. Jake took photographs of the plot and the flat temporary marker identifying it: PETER JOSEPH HARRIGAN, 1933–2005.

The backhoe appeared, crawling toward him down the cemetery road, doing no more than five miles an hour. Jake waved as two workers got down from the rig. They wore jeans and work boots. One was tall and thin with shoulder-length blond hair and a mustache; the other was thick around the middle, with thinning black hair. They introduced themselves as Boris and Ned.

"Not the sort of thing we do very often," the tall man, Boris, said. "Not for criminal justice purposes, anyway."

"Sometimes when someone wants to transfer a loved one to a different site, we move 'im," Ned added. He sipped Starbucks coffee.

"I have a friend who works in Jersey," Boris said, leaning against the backhoe tire. "Once he dug up a casket, there were two bodies in it—*two*."

Ned shrugged. "Joe Bonnano, the mob boss who owned a funeral home, hid his victims by burying their bodies in caskets with a rightful inhabitant—one on top of the other."

"In my friend's case," Ned said, "the funeral home was ripping off the families."

"Fascinating," Jake said. "But don't you have a job to do?"

The backhoe scraped at the earth, stripping off the neat layer of sod that had been laid a week ago. In less than ten minutes, the top of the cement liner that contained the casket was exposed. Boris scrambled into the hole, clipped chains to four metal loops on the liner top, and inserted a pry bar to loosen the epoxy that sealed it shut. He climbed back out and gave Ned a thumbs-up. With the shift of a lever, the backhoe's arm lifted, chains straining against the cement. Boris pried at the seal again; the cover came off and was set down on the nearby lawn of an underground neighbor. This was the reason, Jake knew, that exhumations were done early; no relative of a buried body was likely to turn up.

Boris connected a sling to the backhoe, which lifted the casket out of the cement liner and placed it by the hole. Jake stepped forward.

"No water got in," he said. "Good." He hopped into the grave and scooped soil into small plastic containers.

Ned stared at him. "What are you doing?"

"Getting some soil samples. Six containers: four sides, top, and bottom. Standard procedure. You want to make sure the body hasn't picked up anything from the groundwater."

"Like what?"

"Arsenic, for one thing. People have been wrongly accused of murder because an ME made that mistake. Two Englishmen in the early nineteen hundreds were hanged for poisoning their wives; turned out later that rainwater had washed arsenic from the soil into the coffins."

"Shouldn't that cement box keep everything out?"

Jake climbed back up. "Depends on how much groundwater there is and how well the seal holds. Best to be careful."

He examined the casket. Save for adherent soil, the wood was shiny and clean, as though it had just been lowered into the ground. The court order had mandated he perform the autopsy in situ. He had brought his implements from the car.

Ned unscrewed the lid and Jake gently pushed it open. His heart lunged. Pete's face, ruddy in life, was pale in death. Jake knew it was because of the removal of blood during the embalming. But otherwise it was Pete as he had been in life—dressed in his favorite brown tweed suit, white shirt open at the neck—and the sight of his friend, free from pain, filled Jake with an unexpected poignancy. Maybe the killer had done Pete a favor, but shouldn't that have been Pete's decision? Shouldn't this beloved man have been allowed to live to the last moment, savoring what little time he had left?

Sentimental. You don't know if he was even poisoned or if he killed himself, unlikely as that is. Get to work.

Jake needed to examine Pete's heart to determine whether the death certificate was right in stating *natural causes*; his liver, for evidence of poisoning; and his pancreas, to see if the cancer had spread. He removed Harrigan's jacket and shirt, easy because the mortician had already cut them up the back to make them easier to put on, then his pants, underwear, and socks; Pete wore no shoes. Jake could dissect the organs and remove small pieces for microscopic examination, but the court order forbade his taking any organs from the body.

He made the Y-incision. Pete's heart was in good condition for a heavy-drinking, seventy-two-year-old man. It was not enlarged, and there were few signs of coronary disease. *It wasn't his heart that killed him.* The pancreas was hard and gray, almost completely replaced by the cancer, but there was no evidence it had spread to other organs. And the liver? From the outside, he could see that the capsule was wrinkled, and on section he found the lobules were necrotic. *Significant but not definitive. I'll do a frozen section right away.*

Jake gave Boris and Ned the customary tip. Then, briefly, for the second time, he told his mentor goodbye.

"It's Wally, Dr. Rosen, reporting in. In my new role as Dr. Winnick, aka Sam Spade."

Even the sound of his assistant's voice gave Jake pleasure. "Shoot."

"I think I'm on to something."

"Excellent! What'd you find?"

"I'd rather not say till I'm sure. But I may have to spend another night or two."

It was like Wally to say nothing until he had the full answer. "Take as much time as you want. Are you comfortable?"

"In Turner? Are you nuts?"

Jake hung up, laughing. His door burst open: Pederson, his fury barely contained.

"What the hell do you think you're doing?" His cheeks were bright red, his eyeglasses slipping down the bridge of his nose. *Bad signs.*

"Charlie, it's not what you think."

"It's what I *know*. Stacy called me just now from the lab. Said you checked in a second case under a lab number that doesn't correspond to any of the cases downstairs, autopsy or sign-out. You've been here how long? You know what the rules are covering private work: *never*, without my permission. You're second in charge here. You could hurt both of us."

Jake had expected the rebuke, but its intensity stung. "Let me explain."

"Does it have anything to do with Harrigan?"

"He was poisoned. Murdered. Carbon tetrachloride. I have the frozen liver section right here, under the microscope."

"I don't care if he was bitten to death by grasshoppers. He didn't die in New York City. We have no jurisdiction."

"Actually, we do: a court order obtained by the District Attorney of Queens County."

"You did that without consulting me?"

Jake shrugged. "You wouldn't have consented. And I had to know. What would you have done if you thought your best friend was murdered and the killer was getting away with it?"

Pederson's tone softened. "Let me take a look." He put his eye to Jake's microscope. "Centrilobular necrosis—guess you're right. Sad, but I'm not surprised."

"Not surprised?" The words hit Jake like a bee sting. "What do you mean?"

"Pete wasn't the person you think he was. He was a good forensic pathologist, probably a great one. But I know a few things about him that you don't. It just may be that his past caught up with him."

"He botched a case? Got in trouble as a kid? Be specific."

Pederson sighed. "Leave it alone. If I had pancreatic cancer, I'd want to die. Let him rest." He turned toward the door. "Stick to your job. The morgue doesn't belong to Harrigan, you, or me."

"Charlie, I have to call Elizabeth. It's her right to know."

"And to not know. Why do you want to hurt her? I thought you were his friend." He walked out.

Confusion swirled in Jake's brain like mist. *I was* his friend. *I knew him better than any other man on earth. What did Pederson mean about Pete's past?* He got up and paced his office, trying to reconstruct the years. They had met when Jake was in med school; it was then that their friendship had blossomed. True, Pete hadn't talked much about his childhood or about his own training, but then neither had Jake. The two men worked in the present, lived for the present, and often, when they shared a case, lived for each other. Everything about Pete was open, even transparent. Still, Jake thought, I've been wrong before. I thought my marriage to Marianna meant love forever. Hah! But that was only a few years. With Pete it was decades.

Jake sat down again. *Why didn't Pederson ask about the other sample, the one taken from Mrs. Alessis? Why does he want me to drop the case? Why shouldn't I tell Elizabeth? Does he know anything about the bones?* He rubbed his tired eyes. *I've got to go on, even if it costs me my job. But I'm stymied. Without the bones there are no other leads. Without Elizabeth's cooperation, Pete's murder will go unsolved.*

He picked up the phone. One last chance. "Elizabeth, it's Jake. Bad time?"

"Daniel isn't here, the kids are doing their homework, I'm relaxing for the first time today after the press frenzy at the office. Yes, it's a bad time—that is, if you're calling about Dad."

"I hate to do this, and I wouldn't if it weren't essential. But I may need your help, and if so I need to tell you the truth. Your dad didn't die a natural death from cancer. He was poisoned. Murdered. We exhumed the body this morning. The proof is irrefutable."

There was a long silence. Only the sound of Elizabeth's breathing told him she hadn't hung up. "Maybe you should try living on top of the earth for a while," she said at last, "instead of below it with the other worms."

CHAPTER FOURTEEN

JAKE CALLED Manny's cell, told her he was running thirty minutes late, and asked her to meet him on the steps of his house. Her enthusiastic agreement was the only good news he'd had all day.

She wasn't there. *Shit.* He checked his watch. *Okay, forty-five minutes late. If she'd really wanted to see me, she'd have waited.*

He threw open the door. Someone was cooking.

"Manny?" he called, with a burst of glee. "What's going on?"

Jake heard the sound of paws scrambling on the hardwood floor. A red-furred dog dressed in designer doggie duds careered down the hall and leaped up to the level of his knees. Manny stuck her head out of the kitchen.

"Why is he here?" Jake asked, rumpling Mycroft's head. "What are you doing?"

"You invited me to dinner, remember?"

"True, but what are you doing in my kitchen?"

"Cooking."

Sam emerged from behind her, a swipe of something green across his cheek. "Good thing I happened to pass by when she was sitting on your stoop. Philomena's making us dinner," he explained.

"She cooks?" Jake asked.

"She's an artist."

"Not in my own house," Manny said. "I only cook in other people's houses."

Jake looked at the two of them through narrowed eyes. He'd never seen Manny so relaxed. "I'm in no mood to play house. I've got the headache of a lifetime."

"Wine," said Manny.

"Aspirin," Sam said.

Jake opted for wine. Manny ducked into the kitchen and came back with three glasses and a bottle. "I was telling my mother this morning what a jerk you were to me," she told Jake. "She said a nice girl wouldn't fight with a doctor—a doctor!—who performed an autopsy on a friend. For my penance, she said I had to cook you dinner. And say a novena."

Am I hallucinating? "How did she know about the autopsy?"

"I told her."

"Okay, how did *you* know?"

"Kenneth told me. He was at the Queens courthouse today. Judge Cookson's secretary told *him*."

"Who's Kenneth?"

"Hello," said a female voice, and a man appeared in full makeup, dressed in a sequined dress with a fish-tail train.

I am hallucinating.

"Kenneth is my assistant and my friend," Manny said. "He's dressed like that because he's in a show and because he likes it. He was at Cookson's chambers today for his legal-secretary education course. One thing you learn in my business is that secretaries talk to secretaries, and—"

"You mean, us girls talk to us girls," Kenneth interrupted. Manny continued, unfazed.

"—and Kenneth told Cookson's secretary the gossip about me and you—"

Jake felt his mouth drop open. "Me and you?"

"—so Cookson's secretary told Kenneth about the exhumation order you had the DA request from him. It's that simple."

Jake was stupefied, Manny saw. *Serves him right.* "By the way," she said, "you can forget about the novena. I'm a *retired* Catholic. But I'm making linguine with white clam sauce."

Jake pushed several days' worth of *The New York Times* off a chair and collapsed into it.

"I tried the sauce," Sam said. "It's divine. First she sautéed fresh garlic, Italian parsley, sweet-cream butter, olive oil, and clam juice, and then she added the fresh Manila clams in their shells."

Jake scowled at him. "I thought you were keeping kosher."

Sam shrugged, ponytail wagging. "Times change."

"Got to run now, Manny," Kenneth said. He stepped in front of Jake to offer his hand. His nails, Jake noticed, were longer, redder, and better manicured than Manny's. "It's been heavenly. Soon again."

"Charmed," Jake mumbled, wanting to bite his tongue.

Kenneth let himself out. Manny served the linguine. They ate standing up. It was, Jake had to admit, fantastic. Mycroft seemed to agree, as he gobbled his own portion.

"What in the name of God is that animal wearing?" Jake asked. "It looks like he shops on Madison Avenue."

Manny favored him with a look. "It's called a sweater. It's chilly. Doesn't he look handsome? And unlike someone in this room, at least he doesn't shop at a dumptique."

"Mycroft's named after Sherlock Holmes's older brother," Sam said, through a full mouth. "You remember, the fat, lazy, smarter one."

Manny, who had gone to the kitchen to prepare dessert, stuck her head around the corner, outraged. "He's not fat. He's *brilliant.*"

"He was talking about the character, not your dog," Jake said. "The character's brilliant, too."

"Well, Mycroft Manfreda is *more* brilliant."

I'm not only competing with a dog—I'm competing with M&M's, too! Jake thought.

After dinner, the mood changed. Sam went home. Mycroft disappeared upstairs to do some exploring on his own, and Jake and Manny, comfortable in overstuffed chairs in the living room, were both feeling the disappointment their earlier chatter had pushed back. Jake told her about the results of the exhumation, his last call to Elizabeth, his suspicions about Pederson, and Pederson's mysterious remark about Pete.

"At least we got Judge Bradford to stop the mall," Manny said. "And maybe we can still find some records at Turner Psychiatric."

"If they did hold back some records, they're not there anymore. The guy who breathed on you will have moved or destroyed them by now."

"You're right."

"And if we can't produce the bones, how long will the stay last?"

"A week?"

"If that."

"Shit."

They looked at each other silently, tongue-tied with longing.

Here's her Prince Charming dog back again. Jake gave it a baleful look.

"Mycroft!" Manny was addressing Mycroft in a childlike, singsong voice normally used when talking to infants. "What have you got there? What has Manny's little man got in his teeny-tiny mouth? Come on. Give it to Mommy."

She held out her hand. Mycroft growled at her. "No," she said. "We don't make nasty noises at Mommy. Give it here." She pulled the object from Mycroft's mouth and handed it to Jake. "Did he get this out of the garbage?"

It was a curved piece of bone. He inspected it. "This bone's human. A mandible."

"Human? What kind of pervert leaves human bones in the garbage?"

"He didn't get it from the garbage. It's one of my teaching specimens."

"Why do you leave it lying around?"

"I didn't. They're in storage."

"What do you call that?" She pointed to a very large bone perched atop a filing cabinet in the corner.

"That's a thighbone from an allosaurus. I got it at a dinosaur bone auction."

"Why?"

He shrugged. "I thought it was cool. Looks like a human femur only much bigger. Not only do our bones look alike but more than ninety percent of our DNA is the same."

"I rest my case." She looked at the bone. "At least it's not covered in dust. You must have the best housekeeper in Manhattan."

"She's not allowed to touch the specimens. They're organized to my personal filing system, so I can find what I need when I need it. Everything has educational value. Take the mandible, for instance. I use it to show students how dental records can be used to identify human remains. This one's female. You can tell because it's smoother where the muscles attach to the sides. You can see right off she's had some dental work. Cavities were filled in the first and second molars. And the—"

"What is it?" Manny asked.

He was staring at the bone, a wild light in his eyes. "God!" he cried. "God! You were right! The dog's Mycroft and Sherlock rolled into one."

———

Jake stood and raced up the stairs, Mycroft at his heels.

"Where are you going?" Manny called, following him.

"Fourth floor. Specimen room."

They entered a room Manny suspected had once been a ladies' boudoir. It still had hints of elegance: a marble fireplace, stained-glass panels atop the windows, floral-design moldings below the ceiling. But it was a man's room now—a mad scientist's room—filled with glass jars containing viscera, boxes of hair, a microscope, and what must have been a dozen cartons of bones, sealed and labeled.

Jake rushed to the box marked SKULLS. "Thank the Lord," he breathed.

"That box is taped shut," Manny said. "Mycroft couldn't have gotten the bone from there."

"Precisely, my dear Watson."

He dashed out of the room and up the stairs to the attic. If the specimen room was organized clutter, here there was chaos. Boxes were strewn about the floor as though washed up after a shipwreck; lawn bags full of paper lined the walls; soil had been tracked across the floor.

"Mycroft, fetch!" Jake ordered.

The dog went unerringly to a brown paper bag on the floor and began to scrounge in it. It had been torn open on one side; Manny could see that it was filled with bones.

"Pete," Jake said, grinning, "you brilliant old son of a bitch."

"What's in there?" Manny asked.

"This room contains all the stuff I took from Pete's house. I haven't even begun to go through it. And *this*"—he pointed to the garbage bag—"contains bones we found in the field behind Turner Psychiatric. The important ones, I suspect. Pete must have brought them to his house when he came back from the morgue on the Monday after I left him."

Her eyes widened. "The *Turner* skeletons?"

He radiated excitement. "The Turner skeletons. What your adorable, mother-loving, *brilliant* dog brought us was the mandible from Skeleton Four. I guess the label fell off when Mycroft brought it to us."

Jake's joy was infectious, Manny thought, forgetting for a moment the seriousness of their endeavor. "Why would Harrigan take the bones?" she asked. "Isn't it against procedure?"

"Absolutely. So there was a good reason for him to do it. He must have known the bones were evidence of something—though I'm not sure just what. Anyway, that's why he was murdered. He knew what the bones were evidence *of*, and he might have revealed it."

He picked up the bag, holding his hand over the tear. "Let's go to my office. There's an articulated skeleton there, and we can use it to compare the bones in the bag." He chuckled. "In a former life, Sam used the house for . . . social engagements. One of his companions took it upon herself to slow-dance with the skeleton. So I decided it would be best if no one, including Sam, entered without my permission."

I feel privileged, Manny thought, but why? She felt foolish.

Jake's office was a large comfortable room on the second floor. The walls were covered with framed pictures and documents, clearly arranged with care: a warrant signed by President Abraham Lincoln to pardon a deserter if he took an oath of allegiance to the United States; four autographed pictures of Muhammad Ali, sequentially showing a disintegrating signature; an article by Jake on the neurological effects of punches on boxers' brains. "I think boxing should be banned," Jake said, seeing her interest. "Its whole purpose is to inflict ten seconds' worth of brain damage to your opponent."

At the end of the room was a massive oak desk, so big Manny couldn't imagine how it got through the door. In the far corner stood the skeleton. "It's a real one, from the Ganges River," Jake explained. "The plastic ones they use in medical school may be adequate, but the weight of the bones is all wrong." Although one entire wall was lined with shelves displaying more books, bones, and specimens, the desktop was bare.

Jake set the paper bag on the desk, offering Manny the leather swivel chair. He pulled out samples of hair in separate envelopes, then a thin oval-shaped piece of gray metal.

"What's that?" Manny asked.

"James Lyons had a plate in his skull. Pete found it."

He handed it to her. The plate was perforated with tiny holes; she held it up to the light. *Manny Manfreda, Private Eye.* "There are letters punched into this." She squinted. "A.V.E."

"Probably the initials of the neurosurgeon who inserted it."

She suppressed a shudder. "Why would anyone do that? A plate in the head is bad enough—but an autograph?"

"Skull," Jake corrected. "It's not unheard of. The doctor might have done it so he could be located. More probably, it was out of vanity. Some doctors can't resist playing God. In one of the bodies I autopsied, a surgeon had carved his initials into a lobe of the liver. He was showing off for the operating room nurse."

"That's *assault.* You guys are weird."

"The initials on this plate could come in handy," Jake continued, ignoring her attack.

"You think we can use them to identify the other bodies?"

"That's what I'm hoping. If we can track down the surgeon, or at least his records, maybe he'd know who else was in those graves."

"Why would Lyons have a plate in his head anyway?" Manny asked. "Could he have been in an accident?"

"Sure, but I'm inclined to think it was a treatment for his trauma-induced epilepsy from a war wound."

"By cutting a *hole* in his head?"

"There was once a theory that removing part of the skull could prevent seizures by reducing intracranial pressure. Nobody believes it anymore. The practice is barbaric, like frontal lobotomies." He caressed the metal softly, deep in thought.

That same gentle touch. I can almost feel it.

"Must have been done after he was discharged from the army," Jake went on. "He'd have been rejected otherwise. It's funny. I thought the treatment stopped in the forties. But Lyons fought in Korea. Maybe the army medics continued to use outdated procedures to save money." He began to pace.

When he's thinking, that's what he does. So did Sherlock Holmes.

Jake's voice was the one he used when he was autopsying Mrs. Alessis. "Lyons didn't die right after the plate was put in. The cut bone had been healing for some months."

"Significant?"

"I have no idea." He sat down and took out another bone. "The label's still on this one. It's the first and second cervical vertebrae of Skeleton Three. See, the broken edges are irregular—no healing." Next he pulled out the humerus of Skeleton Two. It looked normal, just like it had the day he and Harrigan had removed it from the ground.

Once more he reached into the bag and held up his discovery. "Skeleton One, the ulna, the forearm bone. And the metacarpal with the anomaly."

"Why would Harrigan save that?"

"We'll have to figure it out."

"Anything else in there?"

"Other bones." He put the remains into a clean banker's box and rubbed his eyes. "There's a safe downstairs. I'll store them overnight."

Manny felt a stab of disappointment. *I'd been hoping—for what?*

"Let's start again in the morning," Jake said. "I'm due a sick day. Do you have the time to help me?"

Time? No. "Try and keep me away."

"Good. I'll tell Sam about tonight and ask him to come over, too. You can go over the other stuff from Pete's house while I get these hair and bone samples to a private lab owned by my friend Hans Galt. I need to take new X-rays, too. Pete never gave me his. And I've got to see a dentist about a mandible."

Meaning he'll be gone while I work with Sam. Such is the detective business.

"How and why could the deaths of four patients at a mental hospital be kept secret for more than forty years?" Manny asked. "Somebody would leak it, no?"

"Not if they wanted to live," Jake said, remembering his last conversation with his friend. "That's the point. Pete knew he was about to die. What was it to him if he knew something he shouldn't? That's why he was killed. And why, by knowing him, we're all in danger."

CHAPTER FIFTEEN

DR. GEOFFREY RENKO was one of the foremost forensic dentists in America. Jake had consulted with him many times on forensic matters and as few times as possible when it came to his own teeth.

The dentist greeted him warmly. "Sit, sit. You're not here for your checkup, I take it."

"Next month," Jake said, struck by how a man so big could have such delicate hands. They were seated in Renko's office. Jake handed him the mandible. "I was wondering if you would take a look at this."

Renko turned it over in his hands. "You have dental records for comparison?"

Jake shook his head.

"The rest of the skull?"

"What you see is all there is."

Renko smiled. "I like a challenge."

"Good, because I'm hoping you can tell me something that might help identify the victim. All I know is that it's a woman in her late teens or early twenties who probably died in the mid-sixties, when she was a patient at the Turner Psychiatric Hospital."

Renko raised his eyebrows. "O-ho. A mental hospital. They're often butchers when it comes to dental care." He took up the mandible. "Bones and teeth are formed when you're young, so we could examine the carbon isotopes to determine whether she spent her childhood eating cane sugar versus beet sugar. That'd narrow down the region where she grew up. Of course, you'd need a nuclear reactor—"

"I hope it doesn't come to that," Jake said, "but it might."

Renko pulled down a magnifying lamp attached to an arm at the corner of the desk and looked at the jawbone with the concentration of a diamond merchant. "Well . . . here's something." He held out the bone for Jake to examine. "See those four fillings on the edges of the teeth? They're Class Three gold-foil between-teeth fillings. Popular in the fifties, before dentists moved to silicate cement and acrylic. If the work was done in the sixties, it was behind the times. And it's amateurish anyway. They got the job done, but it's messy."

"So it might have been a sloppy old guy upstate using outdated materials."

"Or a sloppy young guy. In the sixties, a dental student still had to be able to do this kind of filling to pass the New York State boards."

"Maybe she was from a poor family and had to go to a clinic."

"There were only three dental schools in New York State then: Albany, NYU, and Columbia. Sometimes state institutions like prisons or mental hospitals had a day set aside for students to work on-site."

"You think a dental school would have records that old?"

"Sure, if they have archives. Copies might be in the asylum, too. In either case, it's a needle in a haystack."

"At this point," Jake said, "I'll take what I can get."

"Sam, it's Manny. Office emergency. I'm running a little late."

"I can't talk now."

"Is something wrong?"

"It's yoga hour."

"Why are you doing yoga at Jake's?"

"There's a nice vibe here."

Oh. "Have you even started?"

"Mmmmm."

"I'll come just as soon as I can."

When he entered his office, Jake was stopped by a lawyer in a pin-striped suit, who identified himself as Anthony Travaglini of the Corporation Counsel's office—the city's attorneys. "I'm here to serve you this," he said, handing Jake some paper-clipped documents.

Jake looked at the heading: ELIZABETH MARKIS, ADMINIS-TRATOR OF THE ESTATE OF PETER JOSEPH HARRIGAN, *V.* DR. JACOB ROSEN AND THE CITY OF NEW YORK.

"It demands that you return Dr. Harrigan's possessions to her," Travaglini explained. "She's only seeking the items you took from his house, nothing more."

What's she doing? First she won't let me tell her the truth about her father, and now she won't let me have the things from his house—things she wanted me to have and begged me to pick up. What's happening? Do they know Pete had the bones? Fear went up his spine like fire up a fuse. "What if I say no?" he asked.

"The city won't back you. She's within her rights. She's donated them to the Queens campus of the Catskill Medical School for a library that's going to be named after him. And she's powerful— remember, she's not just Harrigan's daughter, she is a U.S. Attorney."

"Bullshit!" The word was out before his better sense could censor it.

"That's as it may be. Whatever she wants them for, they're hers. Matter of fact, the sheriff's officers are waiting outside your house. Your brother's there, but he won't let them in till you give the okay. Call him, please. You have no choice."

Jake went to his desk and dialed his home number. "Let the sheriff's men in," he told his brother. "Give them Harrigan's boxes on the top floor."

Sam'll understand. I didn't say anything about the box in the basement safe.

CHAPTER SIXTEEN

JAKE CALLED MANNY on her cell just as she was heading
uptown and told her about his encounter with Travaglini. "No
need to meet Sam," he said. "He's gone to a class on Tantric
sex."

She was relieved. Lack of attention to her day job was preying
on her. This would give her a chance to see Mr. Williams about his
whiplash suit against the Fire Department, file the final papers on
the Cabrera deportation case, and catch up on her bookkeeping.
The reward would be a late dinner with Jake.

Her office was in one of those buildings near Wall Street that
accommodate small businesses of every kind. Next door to her a
dentist plied his painful trade (Manny loathed drills); around the
corner was a CPA whose clients seemed to be mostly union organ-
izers; at the far end of the hall was a publicist who handled a rock-
and-roll girls' band given to skimpy costumes even when they were
not onstage. On the frosted glass panel of her door was stenciled in
elegant gold letters:

PHILOMENA MANFREDA
Attorney-at-Law

Her office space consisted of a small room for Kenneth, a larger room for herself, and a window with a view of other windows; when she looked outside she had a hard time telling if it was day or night.

It was, she realized now, night. After her meeting with Williams, she had worked for she knew not how many hours, barely conscious that Kenneth had bid her good night and that, though the lights were on in the building across the street, no people remained to make use of them. She looked at her watch. *Jesus!* She dialed Jake's cell.

"I'm still at the office."

He sighed. "I am, too. You got me just before I was going to call you. Do you mind if we cancel tonight? I'll make it up to you tomorrow."

Not see him? Well—good. She was too tired for banter or for the avalanche of emotions she felt whenever she was with him. Better to grab a salad, get home in time to walk Mycroft, and catch the late-night repeats of the news shows to watch the spectacle of the legal trial du jour.

She stood and stretched, fatigue searing every muscle in her back, and for the first time became aware of the silence. *I must be the last person in the building.*

Last week the thought wouldn't have bothered her, but after Turner Psychiatric it produced a tremor in her stomach, and she hurriedly gathered up her purse and coat.

Someone's in the corridor! She could see his silhouette against the frosted glass of her door. He was standing still—no, bending down now. *To look through the glass?* She imagined his breath on her neck, felt it again viscerally, as though she were still in the Solitude Room. Had he followed her? Did he know she'd met with Jake and Sam after his warning? *Is he going to kill me now?*

Listen! A noise was coming from outside her door. *What is it? A motor. A machine? An electric saw!* Manny stifled a sob and stood paralyzed, her pounding heart so loud she could hear it above the whir of the motor. The shadow moved again, away from her door and out of her vision.

Idiot! It's not a saw; no one's come to cut you to pieces. There's no man outside. It's a woman, the cleaning woman. And she's using a floor polisher, like she does every night at this hour. My office is at the corner; it's where she'd start. She bent down to turn it on.

Tears of gratitude sprang to her eyes. "Oh," she said aloud, and again, "Oh." She put on her coat, wound the straps of her purse firmly over her arm, and—not without a residual shiver of trepidation—opened the door.

Yes, there she was, the cleaning lady, polishing away in front of the office of Terrance Prescott, DDS.

"Good evening," Manny said, proud of the firmness in her voice.

The woman turned. She was wearing a kerchief that covered her hair and face, a baggy floral dress, and—*strange*—Tod's lizard boots. Expensive.

What kind of cleaning lady . . . ?

"Good evening," the woman answered. She left the polisher where it was and walked toward Manny, holding something out as though it were an offering.

A knife!

The light was bright in the corridor; it ricocheted off the steel like sparks from a fire.

Manny whirled, ran, slipped on the polished floor. The woman stood above her, knife poised, hand drawn back behind her head. Manny screamed, screamed, screamed again, the sound reverberating through the corridor, until the woman plunged the knife and Manny could scream no longer.

————

She awoke to bright light and a searing pain in her right thigh. She was in a bed—no doubt about that—but it wasn't her bed at home. Rather, it had the smell and feel of a bed in a—*hospital?*

She opened her eyes. A hospital indeed. "Where am I?" she asked nevertheless, having all her life wanted to say it.

"Saint Vincent's," a voice answered from the foot of the bed.

She raised her head. Dr. Jacob Rosen, in full hospital regalia, was smiling at her. *Must be a nightmare.*

Memories flooded her. Her office, the silhouette, the woman in lizard boots, and the knife—*Oh, God, the knife!* She tried to sit up, but a wave of dizziness pushed her back down. Her mouth felt funny, as though she had been chewing on tweed.

"Lie still," Jake said. He moved to her side and took her hand. *Maybe it's a dream after all.* "A cleaning woman found you and called nine-one-one."

"A cleaning woman? She was the one who—black or white?"

"Black." *A different woman.* "You were on the floor outside your office. You'd been stabbed. There's a gash on your thigh, four–five inches long."

"How'd you know I was here?"

"You had your PDA in your blazer pocket. The EMS called the emergency numbers you've listed and finally got Kenneth Boyd. He called me." Jake shook his head in wonder. "It was quite a conversation."

"Where is he? And has he taken care of Mycroft?"

"He's taking Mycroft to your mother's for the night. Said he can't stand hospitals or the sight of blood. He'll only see you if you're well or if you're dead."

She closed her eyes. "Which am I?"

"Well—or almost well. You'll be in a lot of pain when the drugs wear off, but it's only a flesh wound. You can leave later this morning, and you'll be walking fine in a couple of days." He pulled up a chair. "Feel strong enough to tell me what happened?"

———

Her story was disjointed, partly because of the drugs but more because her mind remembered scattered images rather than a coherent sequence.

"Your attacker," Jake said. "You sure it was a woman?"

"Not really. All she said was *good evening*, and it might have been a falsetto voice. There's the dress, of course, but she wore men's Tod's lizard boots. Unmistakable."

"Right. A man or a woman. Kenneth—"

"He didn't do it!"

Jake laughed. "I'm not implying that he did. But I'm trying to find out whether it was the same person who scared you at Turner. Could have been two separate people."

The comfort of his presence wore away, and she was once again assaulted by the horror of what had happened. The impact of his statement struck her hard. "*Two* attackers?"

"Say, Sheriff Fisk and Marge Crespy."

"You think—?"

His face darkened. "My colleague, Wally Winnick, is in Baxter County trying to find connections. We'll know more when he reports back. All I'm sure of is that he or she or they didn't want to kill you."

"The person at Turner didn't, but the cleaning woman did."

"If she'd wanted to, you'd be dead. The knife could just as easily have gone into your heart as into your thigh. They're trying to scare you off, Manny, and, through you, me." He banged the side of her bed with his fist. "God, how I wish she'd come after me!" *It's my fault she's hurt. I didn't have to get her involved. I wanted her along. I didn't need her.*

"I'm glad she didn't," Manny said softly. He sat with his head bowed; she stroked his arm. "It means I didn't have to wait till tonight for our date to see you."

He tried to smile and couldn't. A nurse came in. "There are two policemen outside, Ms. Manfreda. They want to talk to you about the attack. Are you up to it?"

"I suppose so." The drug was wearing off, she realized. The pain was worse but her mind was clearer. "How did the cops find out about this?" she asked Jake.

"From EMS. They have to report all suspicious injuries."

"Nothing suspicious here. It was an out-and-out crime. What do I tell them?"

"Just say your screams scared the assailant off."

CHAPTER SEVENTEEN

MANNY KNEW, as Jake helped her out of the taxi, that she could have called Kenneth or asked her mother to come stay with her at her apartment, but Jake had invited her to his house—"You'll be safest there"—and she'd accepted. *Who wouldn't?* The EMS had cut off her clothes, so, with becoming modesty on both sides, Jake had bundled her into two hospital gowns and signed the discharge papers.

She was feeling something she had rarely felt before: vulnerability. It felt good to be taken care of. He sat her in one of his leather club chairs in the living room, propped up her feet on a mismatched ottoman, and made her tea.

"I'll get you something else to wear," he told her.

She was still in the hospital gowns. "Have you been hanging around with Kenneth?"

He glanced at her. "Huh?"

"Never mind. Whatever you've got."

He went upstairs.

She sipped her tea and marveled at the fact that she was alive. Her attacker could have killed her—*poof!*—and she would have been just like Mrs. Alessis, her body empty of her being. That others could be responsible for her death was frightening. Control was her strength, and she was learning how little it meant. She'd spent her adult life dealing with human suffering and loss; she'd even assisted at an autopsy. But it was only now, when she'd come so close to her own death, that outrage overcame her. *I'm a human being. How dare they?* She wanted revenge.

Jake came back. *Recompense.* "Try these." He dropped a pair of his pajamas on her lap.

"I thought for sure you'd have your girlfriend's sweatpants."

"No girlfriend. No sweatpants."

Aha.

"I have to go back to the office for a few hours," he said. "We'll order out when I get back. I called Sam to see if he could come over"—

Please, no.

—"but he isn't around. So you'll be alone. Don't open the door to anyone." He looked at her, concerned. "Do you need help putting on the pajamas?"

"I can do it." She tried to stand, fell back. "Ow! I can put on the top, but you better help me with the bottoms."

"Sounds good to me."

Lascivious scientist. She felt a throb of desire. "Turn around."

"Why? I see naked bodies all the time."

"*Dead* naked bodies. Turn around."

"Okay, okay."

Manny slipped out of the hospital gowns, put on the top, and buttoned it. It was maroon with little ivory diamonds on it—*hideous*—but the cotton was smooth, luxurious. She rolled up the sleeves and thought of lying next to him in bed. *The codeine is messing with my head.* "I need help now."

Jake got down on one knee and placed her feet in the legs. *Is he about to propose?*

"I think you need to roll them up," she said.

He pushed them up discreetly so her feet stuck out of the bottoms. His hands touched her calves. She shivered.

"Are you okay?"

"Fine," she squeaked.

"Good. Lean forward and pull them up. Be careful not to put weight on that leg."

She gave her tush a wiggle and tied the cord at the waist. "There."

He looked at her like a man, not a physician.

"Go back to work," she said. "There are bodies waiting for you."

And another when you come back home.

Manny wasn't in the club chair when he got home. The living room was empty.

Terror filled him like poison. *I can't lose her. She's too important.* He didn't try to interpret what *important* meant; he was only aware that his breathing was labored, his panic was making him dizzy, and if she were kidnapped or dead he would have to get a new name, a new life. He could not live with the Jacob Rosen he was now.

"Manny?" he yelled. "Manny!"

A sound from upstairs. It took him a moment to identify it: running water. *She's taking a bath!*

He raced up the stairs, laughing. Yes. The bathroom door was closed. It was definitely water he heard. Manny was singing Kurt Weill's "Mack the Knife" at the top of her lungs.

He pounded on the door. The singing stopped.

"Who is it?"

"Jake. How the hell did you get upstairs?"

"Rocket ship. I needed a bath."

"Very funny. If you get water on those bandages, you'll rip out the stitches. The wound's probably bleeding now from the climb."

She turned off the water. "Actually, no. And I've got my leg hanging over the side of the tub. If I ever decide to quit lawyering, there's a job for me as a contortionist." She giggled. "You should see me."

"I'd like that very much." He turned the doorknob.

"Don't you dare!"

"It was your suggestion." He stood by the door, listening to the sounds of her bathing. Then he heard water running out of the tub. "There are clean towels in the closet," he told her.

"Found them."

"Need help getting down the stairs?"

"I got up them, didn't I?" She hesitated. "Although it might be fun."

She appeared at the kitchen door wearing his pajama bottoms backward and holding a prescription bottle. Her eyes flashed fire.

"Been raiding the medicine cabinet?" he asked calmly.

"As my mother says, if you want to learn the truth about someone, look in their medicine chest and their refrigerator. And now I know the truth about you. The name on the bottle is Marianna Candler Rosen. Is there a little unscientific detail about your life you forgot to tell me? Like you're *married*? I should have known when you opened my car door for me after the Terrell autopsy. I asked you then if you were married because you weren't wearing a ring. Now I know what 'not quite' meant."

"You're angry," he said.

"You're so right, for a change. I should have known better than to get involved with a two-timing lying son of a—"

"Involved with?"

"I didn't say that."

"Of course you did. Don't you listen to yourself?"

"Then I didn't mean it in the way you're taking it. We're involved in a case, not romantically. You, Dr. Rosen, have a good imagination."

"And so, Ms. Manfreda, do you. If you look at the date on the bottle, you'll see it's at least two years old. It should have been thrown out. Marianna and I were divorced a year ago. We were separated a year before that. Do you want a glass of wine?" There was pain in his voice.

"I'm sorry," she said. *Nothing like making a fool of yourself.* "Champagne would be nice. But I'll settle for wine this time."

"Our marriage fell apart in less than a year. It was a marriage of opposites, full of battles. She was funny and hotheaded and never reticent." He smiled at her. "Like you. She worked for a financial newsletter but didn't like it. 'I could walk away from my job and never look back,' she told me before we were married. That's a fantasy of mine, too—walking away—but I know I couldn't do it."

"Neither could I," Manny said, entranced. *No opposites here.*

"No, I suppose not. Anyway, she did walk away from her job after she left me. She met someone in California and lives with him. Cooks dinner, takes his suits to the dry cleaner—that sort of thing."

"*Your* suits could use a trip to the dry cleaner."

He looked down. Some blood from that afternoon's autopsy had landed on his cuff. "Taking them would be a full-time job."

"Maybe we could train Mycroft," she said.

He looked at her hard. "I'll open the Pellegrino and put the takeout in the oven. I hope you like souvlaki."

She realized she was famished. The wound, the threat at Turner, Mycroft's fear, the smells of the autopsy: they all retreated in the presence of the man who was responsible for them. *Food, then sleep. For one night, normalcy.* A warmth spread through her that reminded her of childhood. *I'm comfortable with him.*

Her cell phone rang. She had left it on the table, so she hobbled over to pick it up.

It was her mother, calling from New Jersey, worried. Kenneth had told her what happened and had brought Mycroft over, and of course she didn't mind taking care of him.

Manny was conscious that Jake had returned with their wine and was standing in the doorway, listening. "Yes, I can keep food down," she said in answer to her mother's questions. "Yes, I'm with a doctor. I'm spending the night here."

Jake handed her the wine. "Of course not!" she said. He watched her blush and guessed what her mother had asked.

Manny lowered her voice. "Mommy, please, I can't talk about him now. I'll call you first thing tomorrow. Kiss Mycroft good night for me and tell him I love him. I love you, too, Mommy. Sleep well. Your daughter's fine." She hung up.

"Mommy?" was all Jake said.

She wanted to kill him.

CHAPTER EIGHTEEN

SHE SLEPT in a guest bedroom, waking in pain from time to time not wanting to take any more of the painkiller Jake had placed by her bedside. When she hobbled down to the kitchen in the morning, dressed in chinos and a work shirt he had left for her, her heart was buoyant. His expression was grave.

"How are you feeling?" he asked. He poured her coffee into a mug with fake red blood drops running down its front. Across the blood, black letters blared: CALL THE EXPERTS. SPATTER IS OUR SECOND LANGUAGE.

"Refreshed. Invigorated. Ready for action."

He scowled. "What can I do to persuade you to drop the case?"

"Drop it yourself."

He had actually considered doing just that, to keep her safe. But they both knew so much already that, even if they quit, there would be no guarantee against further attacks. Besides, his obligation to Pete was too strong. He would have to protect her as best he could.

"I want you to take it easy today," he told her. "Go home. Rest. Let your mother stay with you."

She smiled at him. "Yessir, boss."

"I'm serious. I don't know who attacked you at your office, but I have the feeling it was your last warning. Next time they'll strike to kill, particularly if either of us gets closer. So stay home, and for God's sake be careful."

His intensity sobered her. "You be careful, too. What's your plan for the day?"

"I'll see you home and then head for the office. Sometime or other, though, I'll take the hair and bone samples to Hans Galt's lab in Brooklyn. Maybe they can tell us something."

"Will I see you tonight?"

He caught the appeal in her tone. "Of course, but I'm not sure when. I'll call you. Meanwhile, I'll ask Sam to check on you and relieve your mother if she wants to go back to Jersey. I don't want you to move from your apartment."

She bristled. "Look, I told you before. I don't like anybody telling me what I can and can't do."

"I'm not telling you, it's an order. If you don't obey, the team's dissolved."

He means it. She bowed her head. "I'll be good. I promise."

Late that afternoon, Jake went to Galt's lab. He could have done the work at the ME office, but he didn't want Pederson to catch him at it. His boss had told him to use a private lab, so Galt's it was. He took the bone samples down to the X-ray room.

He put on a lead apron, placed the bones on separate metal X-ray cassettes, and, one at a time, put the cassettes on the examining table, the one usually reserved for cadavers, and x-rayed them: the mandible from Skeleton Four, the metal plate from Skeleton Three, the humerus from Two, and the metacarpal and ulna from One. The metacarpal, he noticed for the first time, had an unusual bulge with a small hole in it. *Funny*, he thought, *how even the best-trained eye—mine—can overlook something.* He'd seen it happen to others a hundred times.

He shot the X-rays, developed the films, and examined them on the fluorescent viewing box. The bulge on the left metacarpal was an irregular, almost shaggy-lined bone cyst—osteomyelitis—from which pus would have oozed through the skin of the palm of the left hand during life. He'd have to take a culture—some bacteria and fungi stick around for decades—and then decalcify it, so it could be cut down and made into a slide for further examination under a microscope.

The X-ray of the humerus was obscured by a white blur. *Damn. Something wrong with the film.* He reshot the X-ray and developed it; the blur remained. Jake remembered Harrigan saying he needed to reshoot the X-rays on one of the skeletons because something had gone wrong. *The same shot? Probably.*

He studied the film. With the thousands of X-rays of bodies and bones he'd examined over the years, he'd never seen a white blur like this from any of his own autopsies. *But I've seen it before, an X-ray from a bone in the ME museum on the sixth floor.* His heart quickened. The museum's X-ray dated from the 1930s and was of the mandible of a woman who had worked at the U.S. Radium Dial factory in New Jersey. She and her fellow workers licked the tips of their brushes to make the fine points they needed to paint the glow-in-the-dark watch dials the company featured. *Yes! That was it!* Many of the women developed jaw necrosis and leukemia. The woman had died of it. But this humerus had been taken out of the ground in rural Turner. Farms were there, not factories. *Very strange.* An idea was forming, one so sinister, so unthinkable, he tried to brush it aside, but it stayed with him.

He dialed Hans Galt in his upstairs office. Hans wasn't there, but his assistant, Amy Fontayne, was.

"I need your help," he told her.

"Of course."

"Got any X-ray film? A new box, unopened?"

"A whole cabinet full."

"Good. And bring me a fresh slide, would you?"

Amy came down moments later. She was not yet thirty, he guessed, but there were already lines around her eyes. *Too much staring into microscopes.* He put the humerus on the new cassette and asked Amy to change the settings on the X-ray machine to be more penetrating. He went out of the X-ray room and examined his other specimens, which gave her a chance to take the X-ray, then returned and took the cassette into the darkroom. There he removed the film and put it through the automatic developer and then put the X-ray on the viewing box again.

Weird. Worse than weird. The same white blur obscured the humerus, only it was more pronounced. "Did you change the setting on the X-ray machine?" he asked Amy.

"I didn't touch it."

"Didn't *touch* it?"

"Did I screw up?"

"Tell me once more. You didn't push the X-ray button?"

"No," said Amy. "I'm sorry, Dr. Rosen. I was waiting for you to tell me to go ahead. When you took the film from me, I thought you wanted to see it before I x-rayed the bone."

"My God," he blurted. He pulled the film from the viewing table and held it to the fluorescent ceiling light, praying he'd see something different. "I can't believe this," he said.

"I'm so sorry."

"Amy, you didn't do anything wrong." Jake felt as if his head would burst. "You didn't turn the X-ray machine on, yet here we have an X-ray of the humerus. Can you explain it?"

"No, sir."

"It means the bone took a picture of itself. The radiation released by a radioactive bone is similar to the radiation released by the X-ray machine." He turned to face her, aware that he must seem like a madman.

She took a step back. "You're telling me that bone is—"

"Radioactive." He stared at her, as though needing her verification of something he dared not believe. "That bone is radioactive."

CHAPTER NINETEEN

"THERE'S A GENTLEMAN here named Sam. Says you're expecting him," the doorman told her over the intercom.

Manny and her mother had long since finished breakfast and were reading the *Times*. "Send him up." *Damn Jake. One mother's already here. I don't need him to act like another.*

Sam, dressed in military fatigues, marched in as soon as Rose Manfreda opened the door. "You must be Manny's sister," he said, kissing Rose's hand.

Manny glared at them from the couch. "Oh, brother, Sam, cut it out."

Rose glared back. "Where are your manners, young lady? Sam's a gentleman."

"Runs in his family, Mom, trust me. They have a Ted Bundy gene."

"Now I know where Philomena gets her charm," Sam said. "I've come to protect her, and all I want to do is murder her." He winked at Rose. "Instead, I'll walk the dog. Want to come with me?"

"I don't think we should leave Manny alone."

"We'll double-lock the door. If anyone comes in, she'll bite him and he'll die of rattlesnake venom."

"In that case . . ." Rose reached for her coat.

"Don't come back, either of you," Manny said. "Just give the key to Mycroft. He can let himself in."

When they left, she called her office and asked Kenneth to field all phone calls and fax her the mail. She didn't want to tell him Jake had grounded her, so she simply said she had a stomach flu. He seemed to accept it.

She stretched out on her bed. I'll get to work in a minute, she thought—and fell asleep.

Wally called from Turner just as Jake was saying goodbye to Amy. "I'm coming home," he announced, his voice alive with triumph.

"Find anything?"

"Lots. Fisk's in bed with Reynolds Construction. He's getting ten percent of everything Reynolds makes. Mayor Stevenson doesn't seem to be involved, though he probably knows about it; he's got other sources for kickbacks. Marge Crespy? Straight as a ruler. Anyway, Reynolds will get huge bonuses—all legal and aboveboard—from Wal-Mart and PriceChopper if the mall's finished before next spring, and *only* under those circumstances does Fisk get his reward."

I love this man. "What kind of money you talking about?"

"I don't know the exact amount—the budget's a greater work of fiction than *The Da Vinci Code*—but it's multiple millions to Reynolds, a couple million to Fisk."

Enough to kill for. "You sure of this? You've got proof?"

"Yes and yes. The figures on costs of the mall are public record, distorted downward though they may be. And there's a written agreement between Reynolds and Fisk—a *contract*, Dr. Rosen— sitting in Fisk's safe."

"You've seen the contract?"

"I have a copy of it."

"For God's sake, how?"

"My foot. I knew it would come in handy someday. Seems Fisk's deputy, a Mrs. Bonnie Geller, has a boy born with one leg shorter than the other. Guess who arranged for a specialist to perform the operation that made him all well?"

Of course. "Pete Harrigan."

"Bingo! When I told her Dr. Harrigan was my teacher, that I owed my life to him, we became friends. Okay, I exaggerated his role—I owe my life to *you*—but in the interests of research—"

"Go on."

"Not much more to tell. Bonnie hates Fisk but needs the salary to take care of her boy. Took me all this time to wear her down, but she finally opened up her heart—and his safe." Wally laughed at his own ingenuity. "Proves two maxims of Dr. Harrigan's: Over-confidence leads to carelessness and Never trust your assistant." Another laugh. *He's sky-high.* "That last is good advice for you. I can turn against you at any time."

Pete wasn't right all the time. I'd trust Wally with my life. "Better get back here," Jake said. "If Fisk finds out—"

"I'm on my way. See you in the office tomorrow morning." Wally hung up.

Jake stood in the vestibule of Galt's lab. *I can understand why they didn't want the project held up,* he thought, *but it doesn't explain radioactive bones.*

Manny awoke to a gentle hand shaking her shoulder. *Jake?* She opened her eyes. Her mother was looking at her.

"Dinner's ready."

"What time it?"

"After seven. You've been asleep for nine hours."

Manny sat up, pain coursing through her leg. "I'm not hungry."

"You're eating nevertheless."

There's something special about being babied. "Bring it on."

They had pasta, salad, and a glass of wine, mother and daughter sitting side by side, comfortable in each other's presence. "Best meal I ever ate," said Manny, meaning it. She had been hungry after all.

Rose did the dishes while Manny tried to concentrate on the material Kenneth had sent. *Impossible.* Images of the attack crowded in on her; thank God she had only been warned, not executed. Next time . . . ? She picked up her latest copy of *Vogue.* Fashion was the only thing that could get her mind off her fear.

At eleven, her mother and Mycroft had gone back to New Jersey with Kenneth, and Manny had turned on the news. A suicide bomber had killed seventeen Iraqi special forces and wounded forty-two others in Baghdad.

"Closer to home, a bombing has rocked New York's Upper East Side," the anchorman announced. "Here with that story is reporter Tim Minton. Tim?"

"Less than an hour ago, an explosion shook the house of City Medical Examiner Jacob Rosen—"

A pain sharper than any inflicted on her earlier shot through Manny's system. *No! Not Jake!*

On the screen, Manny saw fire engines and police cars in front of what was surely Jake's house.

"The ground floor is still too hot for firefighters to get inside," Minton continued, "so there's no way to know if Dr. Rosen was at home at the time of the blast. Fire Commissioner Nicholas Gould, a personal friend of Dr. Rosen's, says that the cause might have been a faulty gas line, but he stresses that this is only speculation. Dr. Rosen testified recently in the trial of Mafia hitman Freddy "Big Ears" Francesca, but it's far too early to tell if—"

Manny stood up, winced at the pain, grabbed her keys, and limped away as fast as she could.

CHAPTER TWENTY

THERE ARE MOMENTS in New York when hailing a cab is like finding water in the desert, Manny thought. Not even her doorman could work a miracle; every cab was occupied. *Please, please, please! Please, cab, come!*

Finally a cab pulled up. Manny got in. "I'm in a rush, sir," she urged.

"Who isn't?"

"A bomb went off at the home of a friend of mine—" She could barely get the words out.

He turned to look at her, suddenly interested. "The one uptown?"

"Yes."

"Just heard about it on the radio."

"Then please hurry!"

"You got it."

They drove up the FDR Drive, heading north. Manny leaned back, picturing Jake. *Please, God, not dead—I take back everything I said about him. Please, God, not dead!*

"Don't tempt God," her mother used to say. Well, she was tempting him now—begging him—and if he granted her wish she didn't care about the consequences.

The cabbie left the drive on Ninety-sixth Street, went up First Avenue, and stopped at 103rd Street. "Can't go any farther, lady. Street's blocked."

She threw him a twenty and scrambled out of the cab, ignoring the pain in her leg while she negotiated through a sea of people who had gathered near Jake's house to watch the tragedy. By the time she got to the staging area, yellow police tape was already up and uniformed policemen had formed a cordon to make sure nobody got past. Behind them she could see fire engines, police cars, the mayor, the police commissioner, and—*oh, Lord*—an ambulance. Flashing lights and the wail of sirens gave the scene the feel of a war zone.

There was damage to the outside of Jake's house and its front windows. Jake's city-owned car, the driver's side now crumpled metal, was sitting directly in front of the house. "Let me through!" she shouted. A stretcher sat next to the ambulance. There was a body on it. *A corpse?* With a wail, she pushed under the police tape. A policeman grabbed her arm. "You can't come in here, ma'am."

"I have to!"

"It's a crime scene. No one's allowed in."

"I'm his *wife*!"

She pulled free and made her way to the stretcher. The man on it was covered in blood. She leaned down. *Is he breathing?*

She shrieked and stepped back. Sam! The body was Sam!

"He got it worse than I did," a voice from the side of the stretcher said, "but the doctors say he'll be all right."

Jake's voice, calm and resonant and comforting and dear. She gave a little cry and hugged him, squeezing so hard he grunted.

"Hey," he said. "Careful." But he hugged her just as hard.

May he never let go. May we stay like this forever. After a moment, though, she stepped back to look at him. His face was covered in soot, giving his eyes a charred, hollow, ghostlike appearance. They were directed again toward his brother; she could see worry in them. "Took some shrapnel in the head," he said. "It's not as bad as it looks."

"You're not hurt." A command more than a question.

"Shaken up. Every bone's gonna ache when the shock wears off."

"What happened?"

"I was going to the front door to meet Sam when the bomb exploded. He was still outside. That's why—" His voice broke, and he put a gentle hand on Sam's forehead. "Just lucky. Both of us."

The police commissioner, Lucas Melody, joined them, staring at Manny. "What's she doing here? Who let her in?"

The policeman who had tried to stop her came over. "My fault, sir. She pushed past."

"Actually, I'm to blame," Jake said. "She was just following orders. I told her to get here no matter what." He lowered his voice. "I was afraid my brother would need to make his last will and testament. She's the family lawyer, and—"

"She's his wife," the patrolman said.

Jake looked at Manny, who shrugged. "Yes, my lawyer and my wife," he confirmed.

"Congratulations." Melody seemed dubious. "Talk about a shotgun wedding." He took Jake's arm. "I need to talk to you."

They moved aside.

"A Mafia hit," the commissioner said. "Bomb in the car, meant to go off when you started the motor. The person planting it must have seen your brother arriving and tried to rush the job. He tripped the mechanism; it detonated prematurely."

He's probably right about the bomb but wrong about the hitman, Jake thought. He had testified against mob figures several times before with no aftereffects. The current case wasn't high level, nor was his testimony vital enough to provoke such violence. But it wasn't worth arguing with Melody, at least not yet. First he needed irrefutable proof that the bombing was connected to the Turner skeletons.

He walked back to his brother, Manny next to him. Sam's eyes were open, and his blood-caked lips managed a smile. "I said I'd like a cocktail when I came, but this is ridiculous."

"They're going to take you to Lenox Hill Hospital," Jake told him. "Probably overnight, just for observation. The commissioner's asked me to answer some more questions. I'll come right over as soon as he's finished."

"Are you crazy?" Sam struggled to raise his head. "Is there something wrong with you? You've got a beautiful woman clutching your arm. There's no way you can sleep at home tonight, so you'll have to go to her place. And you want to look after *me*?"

Jake took a long look. Color had come back to his brother's cheeks, and his eyes were bright. "Sam," he said, "you just might be right."

"What are you holding?" Manny asked. "You've had it clutched in your hands ever since I found you." They were sitting on the stoop, waiting for Melody to finish questioning two witnesses about the bombing.

"X-rays." He held an envelope out to her. "I didn't get a chance to study them all at Galt's lab."

She shied away. "The commissioner might be right. This could be a Mafia hit and not have anything to do with the bones at all."

His fingers played around the edges of the envelope. "I don't think so. The bomb in the car was one-directional, a claymore mine. Only the person standing behind the mine would be hurt, because it exploded in that one direction only."

"So our attacker's a soldier? This weapon is military ordnance."

"*Ex*-soldier, probably. Which narrows our suspect list to three hundred fifty thousand."

"Or one. Is Wally still in Turner?"

"On his way home. Why?"

"We could ask him to look up Sheriff Fisk's record. See if he fought in Vietnam."

"Probably we can find out from here," Jake said. "If not, I'm sure Wally'd be glad to go back."

Melody had only a few more questions, and Jake had nothing to add. The police, having secured the area, were leaving; only two patrolmen were standing guard. A third was assigned to drive Manny and Jake anywhere they wanted to go.

Jake stood. "I'd better see about a place to stay."

"Are you crazy?" Manny asked. "You heard your brother. You're coming home with me."

CHAPTER TWENTY-ONE

IT WAS AFTER midnight when they were dropped off at Manny's building. "Good evening, Christopher," Manny chirped to the night doorman, as if she waltzed through the lobby every evening with a tall, sooty man in torn jeans and bloody shoes.

"Nice night, Ms. Manfreda," Christopher said, unfazed.

Jake and Manny took the elevator up. "You live on the thirteenth floor?" he said. "Not superstitious?"

"Very. Almost didn't live here because of it. Are you?"

"Actually, no. I'm a scientist."

They stood in front of her door. Key in hand, she hesitated. *Let him in and my life changes. Do I really want that?* She inserted the key and pushed the door open.

He stood on the threshold, taking in the room. "Small."

"Would you be more comfortable sleeping with Sam at the hospital?"

"I slept with him in the same one-bedroom apartment through medical school, and that's enough. Besides, I'm cold and hungry."

"The Four Seasons has good heating and room service."

"No, thanks. I'm a man of simple tastes."

She glared at him. "When will men ever learn that size doesn't matter?"

"It's just that you have a lot of things in here." Jake eyed wall-to-wall floor-to-ceiling shoe boxes. "Where do you sleep?"

"There." She pointed to a beach-colored panel upon which hung an oil painting by a lawyer-turned-artist of a half-full milk glass. "It's called *Optimism.*" A small white round table piled carefully with fashion magazines stood in front of it.

"You sleep on a painting?"

"It's a Murphy bed, dummy. The panel pulls down. The painting's fastened to the bottom of the bed, and the bed sits on the table—it's known as design." She pulled down the bed, revealing a queen-sized mattress covered with a silk comforter. "Mycroft usually takes up most of the space."

"He sleeps with you?"

"Where else?"

"Some dogs sleep on the floor, in baskets."

"Not Mycroft."

"What'd you do with him?"

"My mother took him back to New Jersey. She doesn't want me walking him yet."

He had forgotten her injured leg. "Oh, I'm sorry. You shouldn't be standing. I should be fetching for you."

"You're not a dog. Can I offer you something? A shower? Food?"

"Shower, then food." *Then?* "Do you actually have a kitchen here?"

"Of course, this is my home." She pulled the screen aside to reveal a bar sink in a small counter, with a microwave above, a picnic-sized refrigerator below, and a toaster.

"This is your kitchen? You have only a microwave?"

"With a microwave you need skill. It's a precision instrument. Ten seconds one way or another and *splat*—we duplicate your explosion. Happened to my spaghetti squash last week."

He walked past her to look in her refrigerator; then, remembering her discussion of refrigerators and medicine chests at his brownstone, turned and said, "May I?"

"Sure, *Mi casa es su casa.*"

"Peanut butter and champagne. That's all you have?"

"Not just any peanut butter. It's Skippy smooth and rosé champagne. Everything I need for a balanced meal: fruit juice with bubbles—the bubbles are so important—and protein."

"But as a meal?"

"Try it for dinner—or are you a chunky person? You might like it instead of some two-pound bloody steak, charred on the outside by temperatures that cremate rather than merely cook the cow."

"Your place is nice. It feels . . . freeing."

"Freeing?"

"There's order and not a lot of baggage."

"I take it that's supposed to be a compliment."

"It is. But personally I'd rather be surrounded with my things. Did I tell you that whoever dies with the most stuff wins?"

"Had to get back to dead people, didn't you?"

"Maybe I better take a shower before my luck runs out."

While he showered, Manny located a pair of sweatpants and a large white T-shirt, once Alex's. When she heard the water stop running, she knocked.

"Yup?"

"I have some clothes. They might not fit great, but—"

Jake opened the door, a towel wrapped around his waist. Manny took in hair, abs, muscles. *Nice. Don't stare.* She handed him the clothes and shut the door quickly.

"Whose were these?" asked Jake, coming out of the bathroom. The sweatpants stopped at mid-calf.

"Old boyfriend."

"And *I* was keeping back information?"

"I would have told you." She turned on the TV.

Jake settled into one of the chairs and watched New York 1 News while she took a shower. There were shots of his town house. Francesca's lawyers were asking for a mistrial because the attack had stirred up sympathy for the state's witness. *Garbage.*

Manny came out of the bathroom wearing silver satin pajamas. She had left the top buttons open, but when she caught Jake's stare she closed them. "Hungry?"

"Yes, but first may I use your bathroom?"

"Sure, but didn't you just—"

"Not for that. I think I can make the vanity into a view box."

"You're going to *work?*" *What is he, a neuter? A castrato? Get a life, man—only not with me.*

"I need to talk to you about something before we . . . eat."

Something more important than sex? "If you promise we'll . . . eat afterward." She sat down facing him.

"Promise. There's something troublesome about the Turner bones. Skeleton Two, the humerus—it's radioactive."

His seriousness shook her. Desire dissolved in fear. "What does it mean?"

"Something strange happened to that person before he died. It's a finding we might see in the victims of Hiroshima or Chernobyl, if they lived long enough. Come, I'll show you."

They squeezed into the bathroom. Jake switched off the overhead light, using the vanity bulbs for illumination. He opened his envelope, put the film of the humerus on the vanity table, and explained how radiation from the bone had developed the image on the film without the use of the X-ray machine. "It means that something radioactive was incorporated in this bone, and this happened before he died." He switched pictures. "And here's the mandible from Skeleton Four. The dental work is bizarre, amateurish. And look"—another picture—"here's the metal plate from Skeleton Three. Lyons. I thought the initials were A.V.E., but that's why I couldn't locate the neurosurgeon. The middle letter's abraded. The real initials are A.W.E.—we'll be able to find him now!"

"Pretty amazing," Manny said, in a flat voice. She had long ago stopped looking at the pictures but was staring at him, and all his words about X-rays and radiation and bones were feeble missiles that failed to reach their target. Now, she knew, he had caught her stare and understood it.

She was remembering something that had happened the year before, after she had hired Jake to do the second autopsy in the Terrell case. The local doctor had picked up the postmortem X-ray of her client's chest and had clipped it onto the light box. Just as the doctor's left hand had left the X-ray, Jake, without a word, had tugged the film off the light box, turned it around, and put it back correctly in one swift motion, simple yet powerful.

There was something in Manny's tone of voice that made Jake look up from the film he was holding. He looked into her eyes and in the next second leaned down and kissed her on the mouth. With precision and skill, he undid the buttons of her silver pajama top— the buttons Manny had so carefully buttoned up—and started to massage her breasts.

"Wait!" Manny said, coming up for air.

"What?"

"Not what. Wait."

"Why? We're both grown-ups."

The sight of the blood in the Alessis autopsy flashed in her head. "Did you wash your hands?"

"Manny!"

"Okay."

He kissed her again. She remembered him holding Mrs. Alessis's heart, drew away, and licked his ear, hoping the pleasure would erase her memory. Then there was the sound of the buzz saw cutting through the skull and the clouds of bone dust around his hands and face.

The movement of her hands had gone from the rpm of a propeller to the speed of a failing engine. "Manny, what's the matter?" asked Jake.

"I'm fine. Do you get yourself checked for diseases?"

He looked down at her. *She's serious.* "Everyone I autopsy is tested for AIDS."

"That's comforting," she chirped, trying to restart the moment. But there was that autopsy image again, in front of her, as if she were hallucinating. "Aren't you a little old for me?"

"You won't be able to keep up."

I love a challenge. "Okay," she whispered, but he didn't hear her.

She was awakened by the ringing of his cell phone. Jake leaped out of bed and grabbed it.

"Hello? . . . Hans . . . Yes, I'm fine. . . . Now? . . . Brooklyn? . . . Can't you tell me on the phone? . . . Okay, okay, I understand. The diner near the lab . . . Give me an hour. . . . Bye."

He sat next to Manny and kissed her hair, grateful to her in ways he knew he could never express. "How would you like to go to Brooklyn for breakfast?"

CHAPTER TWENTY-TWO

HANS GALT was seated at a back booth in the diner, drumming his fingers impatiently on the tabletop. He was a tiny man with fierce eyes under steel-rimmed glasses, a face like a ferret, and graying black hair. He grunted a hello to Jake and glanced suspiciously at Manny, even when Jake said he could trust her with any secret. Before he spoke, he glanced around the room; it was deserted save for a waiter who took their orders for coffee.

He leaned toward them, a finger to his lips. "Experiments," he said.

"What?" said Manny.

"The radioactivity," Jake said, feeling a swell of anger. "Someone was using live people?"

Hans nodded. "It's not just the radioactivity. There's a lot more. But let's start with the humerus."

Jake looked at Manny, who was sitting with her mouth slightly open, breathing rapidly, entranced by this brilliant little man who had shared secrets with him on so many cases in the past. *She's beyond beautiful.* "Okay, start there."

"You know I worked for the Nuclear Regulatory Commission. The humerus contains a higher level of radiation than anything I saw there: strontium ninety. By the nineteen fifties we knew it was one of the most deadly carcinogens on the planet. It still is. Even a minuscule amount can cause bone cancer, leukemia, and soft-tissue malignancies called sarcomas."

He addressed this last to Manny, professor to student. "And the humerus?" she asked.

"Contains more than a minuscule amount. It has a half-life of twenty-nine years, but it can be active in the body for many decades."

"Terrifying," she said. "Where would it come from?"

"Terrorists," Jake answered, "governments—"

"And scientists who make bombs," Hans finished. "It's in the fallout of exploded nuclear devices."

Manny was mystified. "But they weren't making nuclear devices at Turner. It's a mental hospital."

"They weren't *making* them there," Hans said, "but maybe they were testing their effects."

"Human guinea pigs," she breathed.

Hans seemed almost pleased. "It gets worse. We found other things in the samples. The hair of Skeletons Two and Three contained mescaline—again, high levels—and also lysergic acid diethylamide, LSD. And in the hair of Skeleton Four, the woman, there was no LSD but there was mescaline in an amount a hundred times greater than in the other two."

Manny had some expertise. "I know mescaline occurs naturally in the peyote plant and can be synthetically made, and its mind-altering effects can be enhanced by the use of other chemicals. But why at Turner?"

"How do you know so much about drugs?" Jake asked.

"Represented a Native American in a freedom-of-religion case. Used drugs in their rituals."

"Why doesn't that surprise me?" He turned to Hans. "Did you do a segmental analysis?"

"What's that?" asked Manny.

"Body hair is a storehouse for drugs," Jake explained. "Head hair grows about half an inch a month, so we can determine not only if there are drugs or poison present but also when and how many times the substance was taken and in what quantities." He picked off one of her long hairs from her sweat suit and held it to the light. "With this, I could find out every drug you've taken in the last two years."

She threw up her hands. "Innocent!"

"The segmental analysis revealed that Skeletons Two and Three had been getting mescaline for months," Hans continued, oblivious to the byplay. "But Skeleton Four only started receiving it within the last few weeks of her life. She must have been given massive doses."

Manny shuddered. "Poor, poor woman. I'm calling Patrice. She's got to let me go on with the investigation."

"If she doesn't agree, we have enough to go after them ourselves."

"You have more," Hans said. "In Skeleton One: osteomyelitis in the hand bone."

"Bone infection," Jake said.

"The DNA obtainable from the osteomyelitic cavity is from bacteria, *Serratia marcescens,* but a very virulent type of Serratia, one I've never seen before."

"Holy shit!" Jake's eyes were wide.

"Explain," Manny said.

"It's a natural bacterium. Scientists like to play with it in the laboratory, because it's red when it grows in the laboratory and you can easily distinguish it from other bacteria."

There was no pleasure left in Hans's demeanor. "The American government played with Serratia bacteria during the forties and fifties to see if it could be used as a weapon. Sprayed it secretly over areas of San Francisco, painted it on doorknobs and banisters.

Spraying didn't work because too little was inhaled by people on the ground—"

"One of the reasons the anthrax scare is overblown," Jake interrupted.

"—but over the years it's sickened some people who inhaled it. One even died. It's much more prevalent now than it was before the spray."

"It was Serratia that infected the flu vaccine at the Chiron plant in England in 2004," Jake pointed out. "They had to destroy the stockpile and couldn't send any over here. Hence our shortage."

"Some people think the Chiron contamination was part of another experiment," Hans said, "but that's conjecture. What we do know is that *Serratia marcescens*, the type in Skeleton One, is far more aggressive than the strain used in San Francisco. It's a super-bug, Jake, enhanced by humans, the kind that's not supposed to exist. But it does. I saw it yesterday in my petri dish. My guess is the government was using Turner as a lab, with humans for rats. And they sometimes slipped up—hence the bones."

The enormity of what she was hearing set off explosions in Manny's brain. She vowed revenge—legal revenge.

"And it wasn't just at Turner," Hans continued. "The man who oversaw future testing, Sidney Gottlieb, testified about other tests—in secret and under a pseudonym—before the U.S. Senate's Church Committee in 1975. A lot of doctors were involved, including many of the best-known psychiatrists of the day. The top New York State Health Department doctor approved the mind-control experiments, some done in conjunction with other countries. We know of at least two people who died as a result of these experiments: a CIA agent who had been given surreptitious doses of LSD and jumped to his death from a hotel window, and a tennis pro who was given huge doses of mescaline after checking himself into a hospital for depression. Doctors' notes show he never consented to anything. He was clearly being experimented on against his will."

"I remember the case!" Manny said. "The family sued the government, claiming it withheld the information that their son had died because of what they'd done to him."

"Who won?" Jake asked.

"Guess. But damn it, if I'd been the lawyer, there'd have been a different verdict."

"I found the same army mescaline, EA-1298, developed at the Edgewood Arsenal Military Base that allegedly killed that tennis pro in your skeletons," Hans said. "It and other variations are delineated by code numbers that mean *not to be used on humans*. Ha! The world hasn't changed, only the level of the cover-ups."

"Didn't President Nixon order all chemical and bacteriological weapons destroyed?"

Galt's eyes shone. "Glad you asked." He produced a copy of a memo regarding CIA activities at Fort Detrick in Maryland, signed by Donald F. Chamberlain, Inspector General of the United States, and read it aloud:

"On 25 November 1969, President Nixon ordered the Department of Defense to recommend plans for the disposal of existing stocks of bacteriological weapons. On 14 November 1970, he included all toxic weapons. It is our understanding that these materials were destroyed in compliance with President Nixon's directives. *We cannot, however, locate the records that establish this fact.*"

"So for all we know, bacteriological experiments are still going on," Jake said.

"But *why*?" Manny asked. "Our government's not monstrous, at least not most of the time. And even if they were, how could they recruit the scientists to do it?"

"Self-preservation," Hans said. "Enemies were doing mind-control experiments to get our secrets. We had to know how to counteract them. Again, it's nothing new. In the seventeen hundreds, Lord Jeffrey Amherst gave American Indians blankets soaked in smallpox. You might argue that it led to a cure for the disease."

"Or that it killed many Indians." Manny was at her boiling point. She stood. "Come on, Jake. Time to go to work."

"I don't have to go in. Pederson's concerned that since the mob missed me at home, they'll try again at the office. He's given me a few days off until they figure out what to do with me."

"We have our own corpses to worry about. We'll work on *our* investigation." She put a hand on his shoulder. "First, though, home. I'm not going out again without makeup. Thank you, Mr. Galt. I haven't had this much education since the autopsy."

CHAPTER TWENTY-THREE

THEY BOUGHT CHINOS and a sweatshirt for Jake on the way home, then slept for three hours, made love, showered, dressed, and emerged into blazing sunlight. *My idea of a perfect morning,* Manny thought.

"Wouldn't Pete be appalled if he knew the story behind the bones," Jake said. "He took it hard that there was a young woman's skeleton. Imagine how much worse if he'd realized she was poisoned."

They were on the steps of the public library. Manny wanted to see if they could find anything in the Church Committee hearings that would lead back to Turner Psychiatric.

The librarian in the subbasement microfiche room told them she was required to log in any documents they reviewed or copied. "Courtesy of the Patriot Act," she said. "In case you two are terrorists, the government can hunt you down."

"The army sanctioned the mescaline and LSD experiments Hans told us about as early as 1952," Jake said, reading through a file on the period. "Listen to this:

"There is ample evidence in the reports of innumerable interrogations that the Communists were using drugs, physical duress, electric shock and possibly hypnosis against their enemies. With such evidence, it is difficult not to keep from becoming rabid about our apparent laxity. We are forced by this mounting evidence to assume a more aggressive role in the development of these techniques, but must be cautious to maintain strict inviolable control because of the havoc that could be wrought by such techniques in unscrupulous hands.

"Jesus, the guy was a physician. Hadn't he heard of the Hippocratic oath?"

"They put LSD in cigarettes with a tuberculin needle and syringe," Manny exclaimed, looking at the same disc over his shoulder. "Also in ice cream. They even specified the flavor: chocolate."

"To hide the taste of the LSD," Jake said.

Manny remembered the historical information she'd read at the Academie. "Turner had an ice cream parlor and a dairy farm. Do you think—?"

"Could be a coincidence," Jake said. "We need more."

They opened documents at random. Much of the information had been redacted with swipes of a black Magic Marker.

"Imagine what we'd find if we could see everything," Manny commented. "Too bad the Freedom of Information Act doesn't mean what it says." She looked at Jake. He was frowning, preoccupied. "What is it?"

"I'm remembering Pete. He testified for the army in the case of a doctor accused of using curare on his patients, five of whom died. Harrigan was called by the prosecution. But under cross examination by the defense, he surprisingly said he didn't think the curare caused the deaths. He later told me something I consider gospel: 'Science doesn't take sides.' The doctor was acquitted. It says here that curare was one of the drugs the government used in experiments.

"No matter how angry you are, no matter how much it *looks* like there were secret experiments performed at Turner, we still need scientific evidence."

She curtsied. "Yes, your lordship."

They worked through the afternoon, Jake leaving only for a while, to make a brief visit to Sam. They found nothing that directly related to Turner. Jake's cell phone rang. Manny couldn't overhear the conversation, but Jake seemed pleased. He stood. "Commissioner Melody said I could go back home later today. There's a mason coming to fix the wall at five. It won't be habitable, but I'll get some fresh clothes and pick you up for dinner around seven-thirty. Okay?"

She smiled to hide a spasm of alarm. *I'll be alone. Everyone I pass, everyone I talk to, will seem threatening now.* "I'd like to meet you there instead. See that they put your house back right. We'll eat dinner in your neighborhood then go back to my place."

I like her place, Jake thought. "Sounds good."

It's as if nothing ever happened here, thought Manny, walking up the steps to the brownstone. The hole had been bricked in, the damaged cars had been removed, the air was clear of smoke, the street was quiet.

Jake opened the door before she had a chance to knock. "Looking for me out the window?" she asked.

"As a matter of fact, I was looking for anyone who might be looking for you. Melody released my building as a crime scene and removed the guards. This place is unprotected."

She fought back an impulse to turn and run. "Then come home with me. My building has a doorman. We'll be safer there."

"Give me half an hour."

"Why? Aren't you scared?"

"We'll be safe in the cellar."

"The *cellar?*"

"When I saw Sam today—by the way, he's okay and will be out of Lenox Hill in a day or two—he told me he made the sheriff wait outside for a few extra minutes before removing Harrigan's items. As he was on the phone with me, he saw a box that caught his eye. Pete had written my name on it, so he figured it contained things he wanted me to have—mementos from our days together. So he put the box next to the safe, under the autopsy aprons. I want to go through it before we leave."

Sometimes he can be infuriating. We're in danger, and he wants to go through mementos? "Can't it wait?"

"Maybe it isn't just mementos. There may be something in it we need, some clue as to what Pete wanted to share with me before he died."

"Why not take the box with us?"

"Too dangerous. Someone could be watching us even now. Besides, you want to walk into a restaurant carrying specimen jars?"

Stubborn but cute. "Okay, let's get it over with."

The light in the cellar was harsh, reminding Manny of the autopsy room at Baxter Community Hospital. Jake put on a pair of gloves, pried open the box, and lifted out an opaque plastic container. Manny leaned in to read the label:

Specimen 2005, Adam Gardiner. ALCOHOLISM. TUBERCULO-
SIS. HIV/AIDS. Skin from anterior right thigh. Male, age 41.
Date of autopsy 1-29-2005.

"Strange," Jake said. "This is the name of someone who died decades ago, a case Pete and I were discussing when I last saw him alive." He screwed open the top.

Manny jumped back. "What's that smell? And what are those little creatures floating in the fluid?"

He reverted to professor mode. "The smell's formaldehyde, and the creatures are maggots. Most people hate them, but God must like them—he made so many. Forensic scientists love them because they tell us a lot about decedents: what they were eating, time of death, what drugs they were taking, even their DNA. It's pretty simple—you can grind them up in any kitchen blender and then do any laboratory tests needed."

"I think that's disgusting." *The hands that touched me last night touched maggots? I have to get over that?* "Why aren't they dead if they've been in formaldehyde?"

"For one thing, formaldehyde kills the bacteria that would normally kill maggots. That's the reason it's such a good preservative. For years, many brands of women's nail polish contained formaldehyde."

Manny looked at her once perfectly manicured fingers. *Formaldehyde?*

"Charming picture, maggots in a blender. Remind me to bring my own Waring over if ever I should cook here in the future—now that I know what you do with yours."

"Still," Jake said, "it's a peculiar thing for him to leave for me. Unless—"

His hands are trembling. Manny, about to make some wisecrack, changed her mind. "Unless what?"

"Unless he was hiding something he wanted me, and only me, to find after he died."

"So he picked a place so disgusting no one else would look in it?"

"Precisely."

"He was right. Only people named Jake or Damien would want

to put a hand in there, even though gloved." Jake's gloved hand was already in. Manny turned away.

"I've got it!" His dripping hand emerged from the container holding a waterproof bag with an envelope inside it.

"Is it alive?" Manny asked, her head still averted.

"It's a manila envelope. Look."

She turned back. Jake had opened the bag and withdrawn the envelope.

"What's in it?"

"I'll tell you in a minute." Jake's name was written on the envelope. "It was definitely meant for me. That's Pete's handwriting."

Manny wished she shared Jake's excitement. *It won't relate to Turner. Probably has to do with a case they shared.* "Open it."

Jake already had. Inside was a photograph and a folded piece of paper. He handed the picture to Manny and unfolded the paper. "There's something stamped on the top." He squinted. "PROPERTY OF THE PSYCHOANALYTIC ACADEMIE FOR THE BETTERMENT OF LIFE."

Now Manny's hands were shaking. Excitement buzzed in her bloodstream like electricity. "Yes! Lorna told me I was the second person to visit the Academie. I didn't think anything of it at the time. But Harrigan must have been the first."

"It's a dental chart," Jake said, his voice full of wonder, "signed by dental students from Columbia. Renko was right. They were apprentices. Timothy Iras and Martin Lowell." He could barely breathe. "They performed four fillings at Turner: November and December, 1963. The patient's name was Isabella de la Schallier, DOB 13 July 1945. Manny, the mandible showed four fillings. It can't be a coincidence. This is *her* chart. The woman. Skeleton Four."

Shock hit Manny with the force of a bomb blast. *Isabella de la Schallier. I d la S. The initials on the wall in the Solitude Room. Harrigan found her bones!* "But if that's true, it means—"

Jake looked at her, his eyes dark with understanding. "Pete Harrigan knew the name of Skeleton Four but said nothing about it." He shook his head, as though to rid it of demons. "What's in the photograph?"

Manny looked at it for the first time. "It's a picture of a picnic at Turner from the *Baxter County Daily Gazette*. I saw one like it when I went through the files at the Academie. There seem to be doctors and patients out for a stroll. Why would Harrigan hide something like that?"

"Let me see it." Jake practically snatched the clipping from her hand to hold it under the light. His shoulders slumped and he covered his face with his hands. "I can't believe it."

"What? *Tell me!*"

Jake pointed to a young doctor walking by the side of a young woman. "That's Pete in the picture. Pete was at Turner. *He was there!*"

"And the patient," Manny whispered, as sure of this as she was of any hard evidence she had ever used in a trial, "is Isabella de la Schallier."

CHAPTER
TWENTY-FOUR

"WELL, Lorna Meissen knows who I am," said Manny, standing with Jake in front of a thin middle-aged woman who was guarding the reception desk as if it contained gold. "I was here early last week looking at the archives of the Turner Psychiatric Hospital."

"I'm sorry, Ms. Manfreda, but without written approval from our director, Mr. Parklandius, no one is allowed access to our records."

"I went through this last time, ma'am, with Ms. Meissen. You are a designated governmental repository for public documents. I am entitled as a member of the public to see them."

"Not anymore, Ms. Manfreda, and Ms. Meissen is no longer in our employ." *Cruella DeVille.* "We have a new directive, confirmed by our lawyers, that all patient records, no matter how old, are confidential. None can be released without an authorization from the patient or a ruling from the Privacy Board in Washington, D.C."

"But the records have been public a long time."

"That's irrelevant. Archival records are now subject to privacy laws. As a lawyer, you should know that."

"I know nothing of the sort." *Don't hit her.*

"Perhaps Mr. Parklandius can straighten this out," Jake said benignly. "Is he here?"

"I'm afraid not." Her desk phone rang. She listened to the caller silently, then reddened. "It seems Mr. Parklandius *is* in. He's expecting you in the reading room."

The ride up in the open elevator cage was as eerie to Manny as the last. She clutched the same Vuitton bag she had carried then as though it were a buoy. The papers she had borrowed were inside. "Wonder how he knew we were here," she said. "And how they knew I was a lawyer."

Jake grinned. "Lawyers have a special odor, even you. I can smell one coming from fifty feet."

She elbowed him in the ribs. "You're a fine one to talk about smells. Why Parklandius's change of heart, do you think?"

"Because he found out you were a *good* lawyer?"

"Or because he knows what you'll do to his corpse if I kill him."

They walked past the closed door of Mr. Parklandius's office and entered the reading room. It was empty, but the same files Manny had looked through before were again set out on the table. Jake opened the file for 1964 and riffled through it. "Here's the picture of the picnic," he said, comparing the one Pete had left for him, "only it's been cropped. Pete and the woman aren't in it."

"Mysterious," Manny said. "Somebody must have known Harrigan took the original and substituted the cropped one. Too bad there's no photo credit. We might be able to lay our hands on an eyewitness."

A tall lanky man with graying hair and yellow-tinted glasses marched into the room. "Ms. Manfreda, Dr. Rosen, so nice of you to visit." He did not extend his hand. "I'm Charles Parklandius."

"How did you know my name?" Jake asked.

"You were on the front page of the paper yesterday. You see, your notoriety has reached as far as Poughkeepsie." There was no friendliness in his manner. "As for you, Ms. Manfreda, the board voted last night to authorize me to ask the police to issue a warrant for your arrest."

She stared at him. He avoided her eyes. "Arrest? Whatever for?"

"Theft. There's a picture missing from our files: a photograph from the *Baxter County Daily Gazette*. Another had been substituted, but it's been cropped, and we want the original back."

Jake extended the picture. "Ms. Manfreda didn't take it," he said. "The photograph was found among the belongings of Dr. Peter Harrigan, the former chief medical examiner for New York City who died at his home in Turner two weeks ago. We are returning it to you."

"It's true I took an architectural plan when I was last here," Manny said, opening her tote bag. "I did so inadvertently, and I apologize." She placed it on the table. "Call off the cops." *If there's any satisfaction in this, it's watching Parklandius sputter.*

"Dr. Harrigan couldn't have taken the photograph," he said.

Jake shrugged. "I found it among his estate documents."

Parklandius had regained his composure. "Dr. Harrigan had been a member of this foundation since 1963, Dr. Rosen. Indeed, we got him his first job. We placed him at Turner after his residency. Surely he knew we would have *loaned* him anything from the archives."

Pete never mentioned he had been at Turner, and it wasn't on his résumé. He took the clipping, never planning to give it back, and substituted the other. It was meant for me—as what? Jake closed his eyes, remembering Pete's struggle to say something when they met in his house. Sadness swept him like biting wind. *Of course. As a confession.*

"So you see, it's all a misunderstanding," Manny said. "If you don't have me arrested I won't sue you for false arrest. You have everything back, no matter who took it, and no harm done. Nice how that works out, isn't it?" She held out her hand: palm down, *like a bleedin' aristocrat. He looks like he wants to bite it.*

Parklandius left, mumbling.

"Rude man," Manny said. "He didn't say goodbye."

"Still, I don't think we can stay here. I don't think he'd be pleased if we continued to look through the files."

Manny called Kenneth from her cell phone. "You didn't know Kenneth was working for us, did you?" she asked Jake, when she'd finished. "We're all of us sleuths. Isn't that cozy?" She turned serious. "He's been checking into Isabella's dentists, Iras and Lowell. Both are dead—car accidents—one in seventy-two, the other in eighty-four."

"Murdered, you think?"

"I don't know why not. Whoever they are, everyone connected to Turner winds up dead before their time."

"Including us if we don't solve this thing." He started for the door.

She ran after him. "Where are we going?"

"Turner. I want to see Marge Crespy at the Historical Society."

CHAPTER TWENTY-FIVE

JAKE SAT IN the car with his head bowed, staring ahead through pained eyes. Manny wanted to comfort him, hold him, but held back. *He's suffering. It wasn't only Harrigan who died but Jake's vision of him. He needs to bear this alone.*

"Pete must have known about the experiments," he said finally. "Known about them and performed them. He was too young to have acted on his own, but he was involved. My God, how it must have weighed on him! Forty years of keeping secret the worst sin a doctor can commit." He turned to her. "I loved him, Manny. He was my teacher and my spiritual father. I don't know if I can ever forgive him."

"He wanted to confess to you," she said. "That's why he called you back. Not to tell you he had cancer, but about this."

"Cancer of the soul. I wonder if he'd have said anything if we hadn't discovered the bones. He must have realized immediately whose they were and confirmed it by x-raying them. No wonder he didn't send the X-rays to me. He must have destroyed them."

"And somebody destroyed *him*," Manny said quietly. "Don't forget that. Someone must have known Pete Harrigan was ready to talk."

———

Ms. Crespy, it turned out, lived on the top floor of the Historical Society. "You're the doctor from New York," she said to Jake. She was a wiry woman, plainly robust, looking younger than the fifty Jake had originally guessed. "I remember you working with dear Dr. Harrigan." She looked at Manny. "And this is?"

"Philomena Manfreda. I'm a lawyer, helping the daughter of James Lyons, one of the patients whose bones were discovered at the construction site."

Ms. Crespy led them upstairs to her residence, settled them in her living room, and provided them with coffee. "We think we've identified Skeleton Four," Jake said. "The female."

"Her name was Isabella de la Schallier," Manny said, handing her the copy Jake had made of the uncropped photograph before returning it to the Academie. "She was another patient at Turner. She's the one standing with—"

"Dr. Harrigan!" Ms. Crespy was clearly astonished. "I had no idea he was ever at Turner Psychiatric. My goodness, you'd think he'd have said something."

Wally had said she had nothing to do with the kickbacks at the mall site, Jake thought. He was right. "Yes. Do you recognize the young woman?"

She studied the photograph. "No. But there's no reason I should. I socialized with very few of the patients, and this picture was taken more than forty years ago."

"Would the Historical Society have any information about her?" Manny asked. "Maybe something about her death?"

"I don't remember seeing her name in our records. But we have only a few scraggly documents. The Psychoanalytic Academie for the Betterment of Life has more."

"We went there this morning," Jake said. "It's where we got the photo."

Ms. Crespy looked at it again. "I don't know her, I'm afraid." She brightened. "But look. On the path behind her and Dr. Harrigan. I recognize the girl walking by herself."

Hope blazed in Manny's brain. "You do?"

"My goodness, yes. That's Cassandra Collier—when she was a teenager, of course."

"Is she still alive?" asked Jake, his voice rising.

"Alive, if you can call it that. She's a recluse. Lives in her daddy's old house. People here think she's loony, but she's as sane as sunshine. I take food to her now and then, and we talk."

"Will she talk to us?" Manny asked.

"Maybe, maybe not. She's moody."

"Why was she in Turner Psychiatric?"

"Her daddy—Timothy Collier, the well-known gynecologist— institutionalized her after her mother died. Mrs. C was a concert pianist until arthritis crippled her—died of grief, they say."

Get on with it, Manny thought.

"Anyway, Cassandra was evidently a hellion when she was young. Promiscuous in an age when no good girl let a man touch her till she was married. Collier put her in Turner to tame her, not because she was crazy. He was a huge contributor to the hospital— there used to be a Collier Library on the grounds—and they took her in because they needed his patronage. The director wasn't the most ethical man around—"

If you only knew.

"—but they kept the poor girl against her will until her daddy died. Then they couldn't wait to get rid of her."

"She'd know what was going on at the hospital when Isabella de la Schallier died," Jake said, keeping his voice neutral.

"Suspect so."

"But she might not talk to us?"

"I'll bet she will if I introduce you," Ms. Crespy said. She jumped up and started for the door. "Come on, I'll take you. We can swing by the mall site; there's been lots of progress. You seem like nice enough folk, and you were Dr. Harrigan's friends." She sighed. "Cassandra's sure to be home."

"Forgive me," Cassandra Collier said. "I don't entertain, so I can offer you only tea."

It had not taken much of Marge Crespy's persuasion to get her to agree to see Manny and Jake, and the three stood awkwardly in the large foyer of a once-splendid house now sagging in disrepair.

Cassandra was a small woman with luxuriant white hair down to her shoulders and the muscles, Jake noted, of a gymnast. Her eyes were bright, her skin ruddy and wind-tanned, and her hands, peeking out from the sleeves of a bright green wool turtleneck sweater, were those of a young woman.

"Actually, we just had coffee with Ms. Crespy," Manny said, "and we don't want to take much of your time." *If she's insane, I'm a Martian.*

"I have time to spare. Would you like to see the garden?"

We've no choice. She'll talk if we're patient.

Cassandra led them through a living room that seemed to Manny out of an English manor house. A large portrait of a man—her father?—hung over the fireplace; a chandelier blazed light; the leather chairs were scratched but otherwise not worn; the Oriental carpet—an original—had lost none of its opulence. A fraying couch, a pockmarked coffee table, and tattered lampshades over splendid Chinese lamps were the only signs of the passage of time.

"The house was once a showplace," Cassandra explained. "I keep it up as best I can, but it's the garden that gets my main attention. I'm happiest there. You'll see, though, that in the battle between a single woman and nature, nature wins." They went through the back door to the garden.

The trees were oaks, the vines wisteria, rose bushes, the flowers geraniums, impatiens. But there were weeds among them, and a gazebo in the center had partially collapsed.

Cassandra read Manny's gaze. "There's no beauty in destruction. Only sadists like my father think that."

"Ms. Crespy told us something about him—and your history," Manny said. "You've had a hard life."

"He was a hard man. Marge told you he sent me to the mental hospital?"

"Yes. It must have been awful for you."

"It's what we're here to talk to you about," Jake said. "What was going on when you were there?"

She shied back as though he had slapped her. "No, sir. I won't discuss it."

"We think there were crimes committed. Crimes that reach into the present."

"Yes, crimes," she mumbled. "I don't want to think about them." She waved a hand. "Please go away."

"But you're the only one who can tell us—"

"*Go away!*" She fled toward the house.

"Isabella. Isabella de la Schallier," Manny called.

Cassandra stopped, turned. "What did you say?"

"Isabella de la Schallier. She was at Turner when you were."

"We found her bones," Jake said. "Now we need you to help us find out what happened to her."

She approached them, arms out as though sleepwalking, her face a portrait of grief. "You found her bones?"

"Secretly buried in the field behind the hospital."

Cassandra's voice was hushed. "Was anyone buried with her?"

"Yes. Three men."

"Only grown men?"

"Yes."

"Are you sure?"

"Absolutely."

"Isabella and three men. That's all?"

"Yes. Why?"

Cassandra looked down, unwilling to meet their eyes. "Isabella—" she began, then stopped, her voice catching. "You see, Isabella . . . There was a child. . . ." Her voice was a whisper as she gazed into a lost world. "Where is Joseph? Where are the bones of her baby?"

They went back to the living room. Cassandra made them tea and now sat with her eyes lowered, as if she had committed a sinful act herself. Manny and Jake faced her from the couch, both sensing that questions would be counterproductive.

At last Cassandra sighed, a sound of such regret that Manny had to fight back an urge to leave and bother her no longer. *We're subjecting her to something terrible. She's reliving Turner. It's too cruel.* She could tell from his expression that Jake was having similar thoughts.

"It's all right," Cassandra said. "If I didn't want to tell you I wouldn't. A psychiatrist at Turner—one of the rare good men—said that to survive psychic pain you had to confront it." She smiled weakly. "Perhaps better late than never." She walked to the door opening into the garden and stopped there without turning back. When she spoke, her voice was steady and clear.

"I was eighteen when Dad sent me to Turner. The age of majority in the sixties was twenty-one, so I had no choice. It was a hellish place. The doctors and psychiatrists were mostly old men, interested in the patients only as specimens, clay to mold as they wished. The patients were mostly old, too, and most of them were genuinely crazy. One man, younger than the majority, was maybe the craziest of all. He had fought in the Korean War and thought all of us—doctors, nurses, and patients—were the enemy. Often he had to be restrained. When he was untied, he'd explode. And his screams in the night—dreadful."

"James Lyons," Jake said.

She looked at him in surprise. "That's right. I'd forgotten his name. He was one of the few close enough to my age to talk to, but I was kept away from him for my own safety. The doctors didn't want the child of their biggest benefactor hurt.

"God, I was lonely! I'm lonely here, too, sometimes, but I have my garden and the sunlight and I can move about as I please. The cries are the cries of birds; the howling is the wind. It's a pleasant loneliness. No one bothers me."

"And you have Ms. Crespy," Manny said, too brightly.

"Yes. She's someone I can trust. I lost all trust at Turner. The first six months there were so awful I wished for madness. To be imprisoned and sane in such a place is torture worse than a thumbscrew."

She fumbled for control, regained it. "I was saved by Isabella. She was admitted in the summer—my age, and also sane. She was put there by her parents, as I was by my father, only in her case it was that they couldn't afford to keep her and thought a hospital was a better place than their other option, a home for delinquent girls.

"Isabella cried for weeks, because she thought her parents didn't want her and because she was in such great pain from her teeth. That turned out to be a simple thing; she got her cavities filled, and the pain went away. We were put in the same room and were friends from the first. We even learned to laugh."

Her face clouded. "She met one of the new doctors. He was

young, probably not ten years older than she was. He was kind to her; he was the one who arranged to have her teeth fixed. And soon they fell in love."

Manny watched the blood drain from Jake's face. He sat spellbound, his right leg jiggling up and down in his anxiety. "Go on," he said hoarsely.

"I was happy for her, and jealous, too. I recognized their passion for each other and wished I could feel it, too—I never have, you see. When she found out she was pregnant, she was thrilled. She was going to call the baby Joseph if it was a boy, and that's how she referred to it: Joseph."

"What was the doctor's name?" Manny asked, sure of the answer. Jake seemed incapable of speech. "Can you remember?"

"Of course I remember. He was an attractive man, the only doctor at Turner capable of laughter. Dr. Peter Harrigan. Is he still around?"

"He's dead," Jake managed.

"Oh. Too bad." There was no sympathy in her voice. "Soon after Isabella told me she was pregnant, my father died. He left money to the hospital in his will, but not for my upkeep, so I was released, thank God. I visited Isabella a few times right after. Her parents had been killed, died in a grain explosion on the farm upstate where they worked. Dr. Harrigan broke the news to her. She wanted to leave Turner, and had to be restrained and sedated. They put her away, and I never saw her again."

"Put her away?"

"Yes. There was a Seclusion Room at the hospital. Lieutenant Lyons was kept there a lot. They used it for violent patients, though I can't imagine Isabella being violent."

Manny felt chilled. *They wanted to hide what they were doing to her.* "Do you remember who authorized putting her in solitary?"

"Only one man could do that: Dr. Henry Ewing. He was the chief doctor. Mean as all get-out. The other doctors were terrified of him. He's head of the Catskill Medical School now. Talk about rising to the top on the backs of the people you've tormented."

"And Dr. Harrigan?" Manny asked, watching Jake wrestle with what they'd heard.

"Left soon afterward. He never did marry her, never did take her with him. That miserable son of a bitch."

CHAPTER TWENTY-SIX

MANNY DROVE them back to the city. When she tried to talk to Jake, he silenced her with a wave of his hand. "I'm thinking."

"Granted there's lots to think about, but I don't like feeling I'm only your chauffeur. Would the Great Man care to share his thoughts?"

He turned to her, his face haggard and gray. It's what he'll look like in twenty years, Manny thought, if I can't get him on a diet and exercise regimen and if this case doesn't kill him first.

"I'm thinking there's a disconnect. The Pete Harrigan whom Ms. Collier described isn't the Pete I knew."

"He was young then. Couldn't he have simply matured?"

"Not so profoundly. I'm willing to grant he was involved in those experiments, even complicit in the deaths of the people whose bones we found. He might have thought the experiments were necessary, or he was afraid to lose his job, or he was on the track of a cure—flimsy excuses, indefensible but conceivable. What's *inconceivable* is that he would treat Isabella de la Schallier that way—impregnate her and then rush off without taking responsibility for her or the baby."

"Men can be assholes," Manny said, thinking of her own

wounds. "At least most men. That's typical behavior. Why, if you hooked up with me—"

"Don't. No jokes. I knew Pete inside out. He was *fundamentally* decent. Goodness was part of his genetic makeup."

"Maybe he was scared off by the threat of loss of his medical license or even jail."

"Maybe, but he was a fighter. If he loved Isabella and she was carrying his baby, he'd have died protecting them."

Manny glanced at him quizzically. "Then how come he left?"

Jake was sitting up straight, resolute, the fire back in his eyes. "Pete will tell us."

She almost swerved off the road. "What are you talking about?"

"Ever since we left Ms. Collier, I've been wondering why Pete never left a clue about the baby. He left us Isabella's dental records and the *Gazette* picture—clear enough that he and Isabella were together—and a road map to the experiments at the hospital. A full confession of guilt. But silence when it came to the baby."

"Maybe he was too ashamed of what he'd done to admit it even to you."

"Or maybe he wanted to admit it *only* to me. When I opened the box, there'd probably be other people present: Sam or Wally—he didn't know about you, of course. But maybe he wanted to tell me alone, a confession to his best friend and to no one else. Manny, *he's left me another clue.* I'm sure of it."

By the time they reached the outskirts of New York City, they had devised a plan of action. Manny would go to the Catskill Medical School to speak to Dr. Ewing; Jake would stay in New York and look for the information he was convinced Pete had left.

He's probably deluded, poor man, Manny thought, but she said nothing. The change in him was so profound, his excitement so great, his beauty so remarkable, that she wanted him to stay undeterred by doubt. There would be plenty of time after the case was closed for her to assess her feelings—and for him to determine his.

The next morning, after Manny left, Jake called Wally. "Can you meet me for lunch?"

"Delighted, Dr. Rosen. The usual place?"

"No, I don't want to be anywhere Pederson might see me. How about the Carnegie Deli? It won't kill you to eat real food for one meal."

Every time Jake saw Wally, he felt a tingle of pride; this time it was especially true. With Pete's death, Wally was now his closest medical confidant, and he looked forward to a developing relationship during which his colleague's shyness would dissipate and his brilliance would become obvious not only in Jake's office but throughout the forensic pathology community. There are lots of good brain surgeons and heart surgeons, Jake told Wally, but very few top forensic pathologists. The future, he told Wally over pastrami, could be anything Wally wanted to make it.

"I'm flattered, Dr. Rosen," Wally said. "Truly. But you could have saved the praise until you got back to the office. Why'd you ask me to come downtown?"

Jake leaned back, enjoying himself. "Ever spied on anybody?"

Wally's face crimsoned. "When I was in high school, I peeked into the girls' locker room. It was a big deal then. Can you imagine?"

Jake laughed. "No, I mean *really* spied. Like followed somebody without being seen?"

"Yeah." He chuckled. "I am now an experienced private dick. And I have the finesse of a ballerina."

"You may be overqualified." Jake considered. "This time you will mostly be in a car."

"But I don't have a car, remember? You had to rent one when I drove to Turner."

"And very expensive, too. This assignment may take a few days, and I don't want to spring for a rental. You could take mine, though. Manny'll drive me if we have to go upstate. Otherwise, I'm not leaving the city."

Jake leaned forward to take another bite of his sandwich; then his body jerked back. He stood, fumbled in his pocket, and plunked fifty dollars on the table. "That's where it is!" he shouted. *"Of course!"*

"Where are you going?" Wally asked, looking at Jake as though he were certifiable.

"Out."

"But what about the assignment? Who'm I supposed to follow?"

Jake was already halfway to the door. "This is more important."

The more he thought about it, the surer he was that he had guessed Pete's hiding place. *Hide in plain sight.* Well, almost plain. His mind retraced the day they had discovered the other bodies. He had grown ill at the sight of them, particularly the mandible of Skeleton Four—Isabella de la Schallier. *It wasn't because of the cancer. It was because he must have suspected after the top of her skull was dug up Friday morning. He must have had her dental records with him on Saturday and confirmed it was her when the buried jawbone was disinterred.* He had pleaded heat exhaustion, then forgetfullness, gone back to the car twice. *My car.*

Jake willed the subway to go faster. He'd seen Manny's skepticism. Now he wanted her with him, wanted to share his exaltation. He got out at 103rd Street and raced to his parking garage. "I've left something in the car," he told the surprised attendant. "I have to get it."

"You know that's not permitted, Dr. Rosen. I'll have to get it for—"

Jake darted past him and ran down the ramp. He saw his beat-up Olds enclosed in a thicket of new foreign cars. He made his way through, skinning an ankle. He didn't care. He opened the passenger door and with his spare key unlocked the glove compartment. He reached in, rummaged. Tucked in back was something Jake had handled a thousand times, only never in so crucial a moment: an evidence bag.

He drew it out. Pete had left him a letter.

CHAPTER TWENTY-SEVEN

DR. HENRY EWING was in his eighties, Manny figured, but looked nearer sixty. His trim figure, when he rose to shake her hand, was ramrod straight, his face was rosy, his shoes and fingernails polished to the highest gloss. Now he was back behind his desk, Manny sitting across from it.

"You told my assistant it was an emergency, Ms. Manfreda," he said, "but you seem to be in excellent health. I've made room for you in my schedule, but if you're merely here to sell me something—"

"Oh, it's an emergency all right." Manny loathed the man from the moment she introduced herself. She watched him intently. *Spring it on him.* "I'm here at the recommendation of Dr. Peter Harrigan."

A muscle twitched under Ewing's left eye. He selected a paper clip from a bowl on his desk and toyed with it. *Not a bad cover-up but not good enough.* "I haven't heard from Dr. Harrigan in decades. Strange that he would recommend me." *Got him. He talked to Harrigan the Monday before Harrigan died.*

"But you were once colleagues, were you not?"

He shrugged. "Forty years ago. He worked for me."

"Then you're the right Dr. Ewing. It's forty years ago I'm interested in." *I've interrogated tougher witnesses than this. That paper clip's scrap metal. He's limp pasta.* "You see, I've been retained to investigate the death of one Lieutenant James Albert Lyons."

Not a twitch, not a flicker. "Never heard of him. I don't know who you're talking about."

She bore in. "You might not know the name, but you'll surely remember the circumstance. He was one of at least four patients—there may have been more—who died at your hands. For him the murder weapon you used was electroshock experiments. He died of a fracture of the cervical spine."

Touchdown! The hatred in those eyes could burn asbestos. She pressed on. "Still, if you don't remember him, perhaps the name Isabella de la Schallier is familiar. You killed *her* with mescaline, I believe. But here's a question that puzzles me: How come you decided to save her baby? You can tell me, or you can tell the police."

He faced her squarely. "I will not have you sully my reputation at this stage of my life. We weren't in the business of killing people, Ms. Manfreda. Especially not babies."

"So the deaths were accidents? Unfortunate results of vital government testing? Human experiments?"

"Yes."

"And one patient died of strontium poisoning. Didn't you know what would happen if you fed someone strontium ninety?"

"Dr. Harrigan handled the strontium ninety. He fed it to patients in breakfast cereal in different doses."

"And the mescaline?"

"Harrigan wouldn't touch that. He refused. A different doctor did it."

"On whose orders?"

Look at him. He's broken. "I can't tell you that."

"On your orders, right?"

"No."

"Okay, on your orders because you yourself were ordered."

He seemed to shrivel before her eyes. *Like the Wicked Witch of the West.* "I had no choice," he said. "It was a government program. I was a patriot." He laid his head on the desk and closed his eyes. *Waiting for the guillotine.*

"I'm not much of a government fan," Manny said calmly, though her heart was a trip-hammer, "and I've seen more than my share of injustice, but what you did in the government's name at Turner is beyond despicable."

Ewing raised his head. His eyes were vacant. "It wasn't only at Turner, it was all over the country. Remember, this was the Cold War. We were afraid the Russians might use their bombs. We had to know the levels of radiation a person could survive. It was self-defense."

Bullshit. "And the mescaline?"

"The North Koreans used drugs in fifty-two, the Japanese throughout the Second World War, mescaline and all sorts of other mind-benders. Again, we had to know the levels, what a person could be subjected to before he gave up secrets, before he'd betray his country."

"Of course you would never have used radiation or drugs or Serratia as weapons."

A hesitation. "Never. This is America!"

Righteous jerk. "So you experimented on people whose minds were already gone. I'm afraid I don't understand the logic."

"Isabella wasn't insane."

"No, she was just pregnant. I guess that makes it all right. Did you try mescaline on nonpregnant women too? A kind of comparison shopping?" Manny stood, shaking with rage. "This has been *really* informative, Dr. Ewing. I thank you."

He reached out a hand. "Where are you going?"

"To New York. I'm just a simple civil rights attorney, but I suspect a great many people will want to know what happened at Turner—or all over the nation, if you're right in what you say. If I were you, I'd hire a good lawyer. Somebody from the Justice Department would probably be best. His boss's interests might coincide with yours."

She looked at him for one last time, feeling her stomach heave. "Tell me, was it only four?"

He hesistated, then shook his head.

"And their bodies?"

"Buried in the field with the others."

No special day ends without a treat. "I suppose, then, they'll have to stop construction while we dig them up. But don't worry, you probably won't have to give back your Nobel Prize."

When she'd left, he picked up the phone and made a long distance call.

Jake had guessed right. If Pete was carrying something with him, something that would explain the existence of the child, what better place to hide it—where no one but Jake could find it—than in the glove compartment of Jake's car? *Why not give it to me that night? Because he didn't want to be there when I discovered it. He was too ashamed.* He opened the letter. The voice of Isabella de la Schallier rang out across the decades.

> *My dearest beloved,*
> *This is the most painful letter I'll ever write. When you finish it, I ask only for two things: that you do what I ask, agony though I'm sure it will be, and that you keep this letter always as a reminder of my love.*
> *Dr. Ewing told me yesterday that I will be given mescaline. He told me it was for my benefit, that it will help me with my depression, but I know that's a lie. I'm not depressed—you have brought me joy. And I'm not sick, except sick in love. So I will be another of the Turner victims, like Lyons and Millen, Tedesco, Ryan*

and Cochran, and three others whose names I don't know. The ones who disappeared into the Seclusion Room before me. At worst, I will go mad. At best, I shall die.

Of course I refused. I pleaded, begged on my hands and knees. He told me that if I did not cooperate, he would kill the baby—our Joseph. He said that in exchange for my participation, he would let me find a couple to adopt Joseph when he's born—he would even help me if I didn't know anyone myself.

My "treatment" will be long and hard. It's even possible I will survive it, though I doubt that very much. The tragedy is that you will not be at my side to guide me through it. The other condition that Dr. Ewing imposed is that we are never to see each other again. I know you're going to try to save me, and I can't prevent you from trying, except to urge you to heed me. Be at peace. I'm at peace. You are my Godsend, my light, my soul, and my life, and losing you is a different death, a more painful one.

You must promise, my heart. For Joseph's sake and for mine, you must accept what is inevitable. God is more powerful than Dr. Ewing. I believe it is His will to take me to His bosom and to leave you and Joseph on this frail earth to live out your lives in happiness. You are forgiven—by me and by God.

So this is goodbye. It is the heart that animates life. When the murmur of the heart finally ceases, the rest remains silent. I cover you with a thousand million kisses and feel yours in return.

Your Isabella

Pete had attached a note:

Jake,
For God's sake show this to no one. It is a sacred treasure, and I entrust it to your care.

P

A treasure indeed, Jake thought. After Pete guessed who the bones belonged to, he must have swiped the dental records and the photographs from the Academie on Friday afternoon. Maybe he was still hoping it wasn't her, but when the mandible was unearthed Saturday afternoon—bingo. When we discovered the other bones, he had his proof that she had not died in childbirth but had been killed, so he left the note in my glove compartment and hid the dental chart and pictures in "Gardiner's" samples for dual protection. The poor shell of a man. What a shock it must have been. No wonder he was so sick that day. His sins had come back to claim him.

CHAPTER TWENTY-EIGHT

MANNY CALLED Jake's cell phone and told him everything she'd discovered. "I'll go to Haskell Griffith," she said. "He's the best lawyer I know. Fought the government a number of times—even won a few. I'll co-counsel with him. I want to get back at those roaches, those who are still alive. It's personal."

"Where are you calling from?"

"Home."

"You're back in the city?"

"Yes."

"Shit."

"Why? I'm lying here in bed, dressed in a diaphanous La Perla nightgown, waiting for my lover to get his ass across town and fill my bedroom with the intoxicating odor of eau de formaldehyde."

"You'll have to call a different ME," Jake said. "I'm on my way to Albany. I thought if you were still upstate, you could do the investigation with me."

"What investigation?"

"To find Isabella's baby's adoptive parents."

Manny sat up, electrified. "You mean the child's alive?"

"Hardly a child anymore. And I've no idea if he's alive. Still, it's

worth a try. Maybe Pete found him, kept in contact with him, supported him."

"Talk about a needle in a haystack. Couldn't you at least wait to
go until tomorrow morning?"

"I want to get there first thing. I'll find a motel for the night.
Maybe pick up a hot tootsie to keep me company."

"Try it and I'll know. I have the nose of a bloodhound."

"But not, thank goodness, the looks."

"I still say it's a waste of time."

"How many babies were adopted in this area in 1964? It
shouldn't be that difficult."

"*If* the adoptive parents lived in the area, and *if* they still live
there, and *if* they're still alive, and *if* it was a legal adoption. You're
right: shouldn't be difficult at all."

"If I can't find him, it's not so terrible. I'll have only wasted a
day."

"Worse," Manny said. "You'll have wasted a night."

It was a huge haystack. Jake sat in the Hall of Records cursing himself; the task seemed formidable. The Baxter County clerk had
been a friend and admirer of Dr. Harrigan—knew him when he
worked at Turner. Harrigan had told him nice things about Jake.
So when Jake called him and told him he needed to look through
the records as a part of a murder investigation, he readily permitted it. There were over twelve thousand adoptions recorded for
the year 1964. *How would I know the right couple even if I found them?
Did Isabella use Pete's last name?* He looked up "Baby Harrigan."
Nothing. Mostly the babies were listed by their first name. "Baby
Joseph." He riffled through the pages. Twelve Baby Josephs,
though he might have missed a few. Slowly he matched them
with their adoptive parents; if necessary, he'd contact them all.

He took out his notebook and began to jot down names and addresses.

Abbot, Cohen, Fronz, Giordano, Levine, McAuliffe, Murray, Pavlin, Rodgers, Snell, Tracy . . . He raised his head and threw down the pen. The truth hit him with the force a pilot feels when his plane breaks the sound barrier. He raced through the remaining pages, skipping u and v.

There it was. Baby Joseph.

Winnick.

Manny had slept with her previous best lover, Mycroft. Kenneth had brought the precious poodle home from Rose's, and their mutual delight with the reunion was expressed in an orgy of kisses, hugs, and exclamations of delight.

Now, rested and healing nicely, she was determined to spend the day on her own work. She had the Martin settlement conference on her schedule this morning, and it couldn't be adjourned. Kenneth had called early to make sure she wasn't going to be late for court; he would bring the file in the car with him.

The phone rang as she was going out the door.

"Ms. Manfreda?"

"Speaking."

"This is Lawrence Travis in the ME's office. Dr. Rosen called from upstate. He wants to apologize for not calling you himself, but he's at a crime scene where there's no cell service. He needs to show you something important, and then he wants to take you to dinner. He wants you to meet him at Bellevue later—around six o'clock."

Manny would be finished with the Martin hearing by three; it would give her the rest of the afternoon to catch up.

"No problem. In his office?"

"I'm sorry, Ms. Manfreda, could you repeat what you just said?"

"Where does he want me to meet him? At his office?"

"In the morgue. He says he's found something relevant to the bones. I have no idea what he meant, but he said you'd understand."

"I sure do."

The morgue. How exciting.

Dora and Joseph Winnick lived in a small but neatly kept and freshly painted two-story house on a modest farm in Hillsdale, New York, not forty miles from Albany. Jake had no trouble finding it, having been given precise driving instructions. He had called, told them his name, and was greeted with the honor accorded to the Queen of England. Wally's boss? They had heard so much about him; Wally had never been so happy or so fulfilled. Dr. Rosen was welcome. On such short notice, would it be acceptable if they served a simple salad for lunch?

It was more than acceptable, he had assured them, and arrived to find a platter of chicken, meats, and cheeses along with greens, radishes, mushrooms, cucumbers, spectacular bread, and a home-made apple pie, still warm from the oven.

Wonderful people, Jake thought, touched by their generosity and warmth. No wonder Wally's so kind, so giving. He spent much of the meal answering questions about himself; only when he had forced down a second portion of pie was he able to ask about Wally.

"Joseph's brother William—deceased now, alas—worked as a groundskeeper at Turner Hospital," Dora said. She was a birdlike creature in her late seventies with a face, skin, and stance as testaments to a life lived mainly outdoors. "Joseph and I couldn't have children of our own. One day a Dr. Ewing called—the dearest man—and asked if we were interested in adopting a newborn baby."

Joseph, tall, lean, and equally weathered, took his wife's hand. "Seems William had mentioned our plight to Dr. Ewing. Warned us that the child had a physical defect, a clubfoot, but was sound of mind and heart. Would we like to visit the hospital and see him?"

Dora's eyes sparkled at the memory. "He had the sweetest face! Couldn't have been a month old, but he waved his little hands at us, as though to say hello, and I picked him up, and—well, he just seemed to *fit*."

"We didn't care about the clubfoot, and even if we did, we didn't have the money to fix it," Joseph said, continuing the narrative seamlessly, as though the two had rehearsed it. "We knew the boy'd have some problems, but is there a human being in the world who doesn't?"

Dora looked at Jake, almost daring him to disagree. "It made us cherish him all the more. He got teased at school something awful—made him a loner, I think—leastways he didn't have many friends when he was little and no girlfriends in high school, but he was always so good-natured, so uncomplaining, that we didn't really worry about him."

It was Joseph's turn. "It was his brains saved him. Wally could read by the time he was five, and I don't think he's stopped reading since. But he was at loose ends when he finished Columbia Medical School. I think he wanted to get even farther away from people, so he went out to Santa Fe and worked there with kids less fortunate than he."

With children more handicapped than he was.

"Then he got enough gumption to come back to New York City," Dora said. "Think how brave that was. Not only to come back but to practice medicine in a city environment, surrounded by other health-care professionals."

Brave indeed. "Did you ever locate his birth parents?"

"My goodness, yes!" Dora exclaimed, as though the question surprised her. "His birth father, that is. The mother died in childbirth."

Jake held his breath. "What was his name?"

"Why, Peter Harrigan. Didn't Dr. Harrigan tell you Wally was adopted?"

"He did, only he didn't tell me he was the father."

"Strange," Joseph said. "Pete was right fond of the boy. Maybe he was afraid you'd tell Wally."

Pete? "Then you knew Dr. Harrigan personally?"

"Of course! He was Wally's teacher when Wally came to New York. He contacted us then but made us promise not to tell Wally who he was until he had passed his class. Pete had married and had a daughter. He didn't want his new family to know about his past life, or Wally to know he was his father's pupil. He's the one who told us about Wally's birth mother. He loved her, he said, and, as I say, she died in childbirth before they could be married. He and Wally got along real well. They didn't see each other all that often, but when Pete came, he and Wally'd have these long talks about medicine and about life. And of course he got him the job with you. Said you were his best friend."

I was. We had those same talks. Pete must have found the Winnicks the same way I did. And his lie was a gentle one. Jake felt a catch in his throat. The emotion he had held in abeyance since his arrival threatened to overflow, and he asked his hosts to direct him to the bathroom, where he washed his face and stood with his hands on the sink until he had mastered his feelings. *Ewing kept his promise; there's humanity even in monsters. And Pete—Pete was a good man. At least he tried to make up for his sins in the only way he could—through Wally. He's served his penance. I can love him again, even if I can't forgive him for the experiments at Turner.*

He returned to the dining area. Dora had cleared the dishes;

Joseph had stepped outside for a cigarette but reentered when he saw Jake.

"I'm afraid I've terrible news," he told them gently. "Pete's dead."

"No!" Dora covered her mouth with her apron. "When? And why didn't Wally tell us?"

"Two weeks ago. Pete had cancer, and maybe Wally didn't want to upset you."

"Did Dr. Harrigan suffer?" Joseph asked.

"Only at the end. I saw him just before he died. We talked about Wally."

"God rest his soul," Dora whispered. "Thank you for telling us."

Jake shook Joseph's hand and kissed Dora. "And thank *you*," he said as he left, "for being such good parents."

It was after two. Jake called Manny. Kenneth picked up and told him the Martin hearing was lasting longer than expected and he wasn't sure what time she'd get back. "But she's definitely coming in. You wouldn't *believe* the pileup of papers."

"As a matter of fact, I would," Jake said, thinking with horror about his own desk and what awaited him when Pederson gave him clearance to return.

Should I tell Elizabeth about the child? Pete never told her. Why should I play messenger? He sat in his car without starting the motor. *Because she could be hurt by this professionally, if it's revealed publically and she's in the dark. Pete would have wanted me to take care of her. She's Wally's half sister, but she's Pete's daughter, first.* He called her office. She hadn't come in today, a woman with the voice of a drill sergeant told him. In fact, she hadn't been in all week. Ever since her husband had been hurt in an automobile accident.

Good. It'll be easier to talk to her at home.

The Markis house, fronted by a circular driveway cut through immaculate grass, looked as much like feudal England as twenty-first-century New Jersey. Jake had never been here before; Elizabeth had been living far more modestly when he dated her. Now he registered only that it seemed far too grand to be inhabited by anyone he knew except the mayor, an impression verified by a marble foyer, circular stairs leading to the heavens, and a butler in uniform who asked him if he was expected.

"No," said Jake, who had purposely not heralded his arrival, fearing she would not let him come, "but this is an emergency. I'm Jacob Rosen, a friend of her late father's and medical examiner for New York City."

This last seemed to work, for the butler gave a little bow and went upstairs. Soon Elizabeth appeared, dressed in a simple black sheath. *Manny would know the designer.* "Jake," she said, her tone frosty. "This is a surprise."

"I'm sorry to intrude. Truly. But I've found out things about your father you ought to know."

"About his death? I told you I'm not—"

"About his life. His early life."

She sighed. "I can't spare much time. Daniel is hurt, you know."

"Your office told me. An automobile accident?"

"Yes. A truck exploded on the Jersey Turnpike. He got caught in the blast. A broken rib, cuts and bruises—he can hardly walk—and the noise temporarily deafened him. He still can't hear."

"I'm so sorry. Do you want me to take a look at him?"

She glanced at him scornfully. "We have our own doctor. Why don't we go into the library? It's comfortable there."

He followed her through heavy oak doors into a room that

seemed to Jake larger than the reading rooms of most New York branch libraries, where they sat facing each other in two identical wing chairs.

"Did your father say anything to you when you visited him before he died?" Jake asked. "Anything he hadn't told you before?"

She hesitated. "No. Why?"

"Because when I saw him I thought he wanted to confess to me."

"Confess what?"

"I didn't know. It's what prompted my question to you."

"He only told me he was dying of cancer."

I'll bet that's not all.

Her eyes were steely, suspicious. "Yes. Mom told us. Her name was Isabella. She was a nurse at a hospital where he worked in upstate New York."

"Turner."

"That's right. Died of pneumonia, Dad said."

"Did you know Pete and Isabella had a child?"

Her head snapped back. "A child?"

"Yes, a boy. Congratulations. You have a brother—a half-brother."

Her expression grew fearful. *I wonder why.* "The boy's alive?"

"The *man's* alive, very much so."

"You're sure?"

"Positive. He works for me. Would you like to meet him?"

"He—he *works* for you?"

"Yes. He's a doctor. His name's Dr. Walter Winnick—Winnick's the name of his adoptive parents. Pete recommended him to me, and I took him on. He's loyal and hard-working. Invaluable."

She bit her lip so hard it turned white, but she met his eyes. "I'd love to meet him. Maybe after the Monmouth case is closed, and after the elections."

"That would be fine. You intend to run for governor?"

"I don't know. The feelers are out. It's a question of fund-raising."

"Good luck, Elizabeth. I mean that sincerely."

"Thanks. Is that all you have to tell me?"

"For the moment. Whatever else can wait."

She stood. "Then—"

The door behind them opened. Elizabeth wheeled, her face red with fury. "Not now!" she shouted.

Too late. Jake had turned also. Daniel Markis was at the door, and Jake got a good look at him. His face was unblemished, his stance upright. He was dressed in slacks and a sports shirt. *Can hardly walk? I've never seen a man beat it so fast in all my life. Markis isn't bedridden, but he may be deaf; Elizabeth had to shout.* He faced her. She cowered. *All right. Gloves off.* He grabbed her arm.

"Let go!" she screamed. "What are you doing?"

"Making you listen. When you see your half brother, Elizabeth, don't be too upset. He has a clubfoot, you see. When you give a pregnant woman mescaline, deformities to the fetus are inevitable. Pete didn't tell you the whole truth. She wasn't a nurse, she was a patient. And she didn't die of pneumonia. She died of mescaline poisoning. And your father was involved with the program that administered it."

She screamed again, the sound reverberating through the room. He heard a car door open and close, the sound of tires on gravel. *If you set off a claymore mine from behind, the unidirectional balls don't hit you but the blast'll damage the auditory nerve. That's what happened to Markis!* He raced past Elizabeth, pushed aside the butler who appeared in the doorway, and dashed to his car. *Markis was that "woman." Elizabeth must have known. My God.*

He called Manny's office from the car.

"Ms. Manfreda's office."

Shit. Kenneth. "Where's Manny?"

"She came back from court early and left half an hour ago. Went to do some shopping—she says her clothes are *rags*—and then she was going to meet you, as requested, at the morgue. Another romantic rendezvous among the corpses, I gathered. She was so excited about her afternoon—she could make the trunk shows at Bergdorf's—she left her cell phone on her desk."

"Me? What are you talking about?"

"She said someone from your office called and told her to meet you at Bellevue, in the morgue, later this afternoon. Said you'd found something and wanted to show it to her there."

Jake felt cold fear settle in the pit of his stomach.

CHAPTER TWENTY-NINE

A MAN IN A hospital coat came up to her in the Bellevue lobby, wearing a Secret Service–type transmitter in his ear. "Ms. Manfreda?"

"Yes."

"I'm Lawrence Travis. Dr. Rosen asked me to escort you to the morgue. He's in an urgent meeting he couldn't avoid, but he'll meet you as soon as he's finished."

He's probably with Pederson, deciding his fate. "I can find the morgue easily enough. No need to come with me."

"It's no trouble. It's the old morgue, a creepy place. I promise you'll be grateful for the company."

She smiled. "Thank you. That's very nice of you."

They took the elevator to the basement, where he led her down a cheerless, brightly lit corridor until they came to a door. She shivered. "It's cold down here."

"It'll be warmer inside," Travis said. He opened the door. Manny saw a wall of numbered silver metal boxes, four boxes high and about fifteen rows wide.

A gurney holding a corpse stood in front of them.

"This is where we keep the bodies until the funeral director picks them up or they go to potter's field," Travis explained as they

— 218 —

entered. "We refrigerate the bodies that have to remain here for a while. They're on trays in the drawers at the back. One body per tray, about half of them in use at any one time, unless there's been a disaster and the corpses pile up."

He's enjoying himself. Creepy is right.

"All unidentified and unclaimed bodies in Manhattan end up here before going to Hart Island for burial. Can't recognize most of them—they're too decayed. Many are old people who've outlived their friends and relatives. The police have a Missing Persons Bureau office in the back there, next to the old autopsy room. It's hardly ever manned, though."

"The old autopsy room? Is that where Dr. Rosen wants to meet me?" He didn't answer her. She asked again.

"I guess so. He just told me the old morgue."

"Since there's an old one, there must be a new one. Why wouldn't he meet me there?"

Travis shrugged. "You'll have to ask him. This used to be the ME morgue, but now they're across the street in their own building, where Dr. Rosen works."

Suspicion leeched into her brain. "Have you been working for Dr. Rosen a long time?"

"No, ma'am. Three–four weeks is all. I heard him give a lecture on blood splatter and decided he was the person I wanted to be transferred to."

Manny's ears tingled. "A lecture on what?"

"Blood splatter."

Blood splatter. Jake's laughed a dozen times at laymen who make that mistake: "Splatter is a sound, not the description of blood evidence. Spatter is the word for evidence." This man's never been to Jake's lecture. This man's not with the ME's office. She turned to face him, fear whipping at her like a cold wind. She looked intently at his feet. Through his paper booties she could see lizard boots. *It's the same person who attacked me outside my office!*

"I warned you, Ms. Manfreda, not to continue your investigation."

She had felt his breath before—at Turner. "Who are you?" she whispered.

"Daniel Markis." His voice was unnaturally loud.

"Elizabeth's husband!" Manny understood. Jake had told her Markis was in Elizabeth's thrall, so much in her shadow he was practically invisible. She must have sent him to Turner; he was the "cleaning lady" outside her office. "Jake says you're a high school football coach."

"What?"

She raised her voice. "A high school coach."

He grinned. "Among other things. Mostly, I work for my wife."

A knife glinted in his hand. She recognized it with a spasm of terror. "I spared you on Elizabeth's orders," he said. "We had to kill Pete—he *knew*—but she thought you and Jake should live. Just so long as you dropped the investigation. A sentimental mistake. A mistake we aren't prepared to make twice," he hissed, stepping toward her.

"Help!" Her shout echoed off the trays. "*Help!*" Jake, Rose, Kenneth, Mycroft—their faces were vivid in her brain, and Manny was empowered by their love.

She screamed and slammed the gurney into him, and he fell to the ground backward, momentarily dazed.

"You little bitch!" he howled, as he struggled to stand up.

She ducked behind the first row of metal boxes, stumbling on her high heels. She took off her shoes, barely registering that they were the same ones she had worn to the Carramia trial, and held them as she edged toward the body refrigeration unit. She grabbed the handle of one of the boxes, opened it, climbed onto the tray, then pulled it closed from the inside. A corpse stared at her through decomposing eyes, and she dug her fingernails into her palms to keep from screaming.

She could hear Markis approach. "Where are you, bitch?"

Inside it was one big cold storage refrigerator with no barriers. She could move between the many trays in the massive refrigeration unit, impeded only by dead bodies. Maybe Markis didn't know this. She moved to another tray, its inhabitant covered by a sheet. Markis pulled out the drawer she had just left, then another and another. "You can't hide for long," he muttered. She felt the anger of his frustration.

She crawled to another tray, one level up, the hum of the refrigerator unit masking the noise. Her clothes were wet with decomposition fluids from the bodies; the stench of decaying flesh was awful.

She could hear Markis coming closer and darted to an empty drawer on the other side of the unit. She heard another drawer open and slam shut. She moved to another tray. As the drawer was opened she was unable to see him in the gloom.

Then his hands were around her throat—ice-cold hands, a corpse's hands—and he was choking her. "This way is better," he whispered. "No knife wound, no marks. I'll put you in a body bag and you'll be no different from any of the other bodies. You'll be buried in potter's field with the rest of them."

Markis's fingers tightened. Dizzy, unable to breathe, she let one of her shoes drop from her hand but gripped the other with desperate strength and slammed it into the top of his skull. Metal heel met bone. He groaned and she felt his hands relax; warm blood dropped from his head across her face. He stepped back into the light and slowly crumpled, her prized stiletto sticking out of the top of his head. She gulped air, gulped again, closed her eyes.

A sound. A gust of warm air. His breath? No, air from the outside corridor. A doctor limped to her side, two Bellevue security guards in tow. "Are you all right?" he asked, his eyes wide with anxiety. "Dr. Rosen told me to follow you, but I went to the new morgue, not this one." She managed a smile. Wally, she realized.

Kenneth rushed in, mouthed the words "product placement," then fainted dead away. Then, finally, Jake was at the door, his joy fresher than the air they breathed. He took a step toward her, arms outstretched. She fended him off with a mock glare.

"I know you'd be late for your own funeral. But couldn't you have tried to be on time for mine?"

CHAPTER THIRTY

"Spinosa had it right: *Ambition is a species of madness*," Jake said. "In Elizabeth's case, the madness was extreme—it led to patricide." Proud of his erudition, Jake glanced at Manny to see if she was impressed.

"Didn't he say the same thing about lust?" she asked, keeping her eyes steadfastly on the road.

One-upped. "God knows my lust is madness."

She gave his knee a squeeze. "Mine seems to me perfectly sane."

They were driving to Turner once more, Manny at the wheel, Mycroft in Jake's lap: "For a date with Sheriff Fisk," he had announced when he'd asked her if she wanted to come along, "only he doesn't know we're coming." She had wholeheartedly agreed.

"It was more than just ambition," Jake went on. "She's about the coldest woman I've ever met, and my guess is it stemmed from her childhood. She probably got the mothering she needed, but not the fathering."

"That doesn't jibe. He was compassionate, loving, a good husband to Dolores, a marvelous friend to you, and he never forgot he was Wally's father."

Jake had spent the previous night thinking it through. "I think he poured all his love onto his son, even before he traced him to the

Winnicks, as compensation for his shame. Another child, even of a different sex, was tough for him. He might have been afraid of loving her too much when she was little, afraid he'd lose her like he lost Isabella and Wally, so he kept distant and she turned against him. It made it easier for her to kill him. After all, he was dying anyway. She just hurried it along."

They had reached the outskirts of Turner. The autumn leaves still retained their color, but today she was too engrossed in his words to notice them. "You could be right; it makes psychological sense."

"There's one thing more. Let's assume Hans Galt is right and bacteriological experiments, at least, are still going on. Elizabeth spent much of her career at the Justice Department. She could have known about the experiments or covered them up by sitting on the evidence. Pete's discovery of the radioactive bones—her *father's* discovery—might have quickly led to her."

She shuddered. "It's too horrible, but possible all the same. Dr. Ewing told me he was following government orders. Maybe she was, too. You know how I am about government conspiracies."

"Or maybe, Manny, it was only about family. Poor Wally. He's taken a leave of absence after learning about all of this. Gone back to Santa Fe for a while."

She glanced at him. His expression was the same as it had been in the autopsy room with Mrs. Alessis's body; now she realized he could dissect facts as well as flesh. *Not a geeky scientist—a sexy scientist!*

"Why did she ask you to clean out Pete's study? Anybody could have done it, and look what it led to."

Jake had asked himself the same question. "To deflect me. I was the only person who might not have bought the cancer story, so to her, asking my help was an indication of her innocence. Remember, she didn't know Pete had the bones in his possession." He smiled at her, noting how relaxed she was—*amazing, after all she's been through*—and felt a warrior's urge to keep her from further harm.

"But she did know about the bones themselves," Manny said.

"Yes. Pete must have told her about them when she visited him just before he died. He was going to confess to me; surely he confessed to her, his child. It was a last-minute attempt to get close to her."

"So she poisoned him."

"She knew about the experiments, about Isabella, maybe even about Wally. If any part of the story got out about her own involvement, her cover-up, her political career was finished. She was afraid it would destroy her future." He looked at Manny again. She was frowning, but her hair—black today—shone in the morning sunshine, and he thought she'd never been so beautiful. She'd told him she'd decided on black hair to go with her black Sevens jeans and cropped-leather Gaultier jacket over a black T-shirt.

"We may never know if she put the poison in the scotch bottle or if Markis did," he continued. "Both Markis and Elizabeth knew that the jaundice in Pete's eyes from the cancer would conceal the jaundice created by the poison. My guess is she did it after Markis went home. She had a lot of experience learning the 'how-to' of murder because of her position as a prosecutor for so many years. For sure Markis was the 'son' who showed up at Shady Briar, and certainly she used Markis to scare you. Among other things, you didn't know what he looked like and you might have recognized her face, however disguised, from television."

"I'll see *his* face in my nightmares. And Ewing's. The press is already clammering for a new, full investigation. The fact that they've embraced the story may cause the Senate to open new hearings. That phone call he made to Elizabeth's private line after I left his office may just damn him. They won't rest until Ewing does a perp walk on murder charges. And if we find other bones . . .

"And I'm positive I can persuade Patrice to reopen the Lyons case. There's nobody to threaten her now, and she deserves every penny she can get."

A good brain in a great body, Jake thought. "As do you," Jake said. "You're in desperate need of new clothing."

She didn't take the bait.

"Mycroft's discovery of that bone in my study really caused a hulabaloo, huh?"

"Mycroft, Daddy's complimenting you!"

Daddy? I'm now the dog's daddy, Jake thought.

"What'll happen to Markis when he gets unhandcuffed from that hospital bed—and to Elizabeth?"

"You're the lawyer; you tell me."

"With our testimony, Markis will be in the pen for the bombing and stabbing for years. Elizabeth is another story. It'll be damn hard to prove she's guilty of murder unless Markis dimes her out. So far, he's not talking or can't talk. Her political career's finished, of course, but full justice—well, we'll have to wait and see."

"Don't you want to go after her? After all, you're well known in New Jersey now because of the Carramia case; any judge will be glad to hear you out again."

"I lost that case, you turncoat!"

He grinned. "I know. But this time I'll be *your* star witness."

Manny parked at the mall site. State troopers were combing through the area while several people, including Ms. Crespy, stood to the side, watching. "They'll use ground-penetrating radar to find the other victims," Jake said. "Needless to say, the mall's been postponed indefinitely." He helped Manny out of the car. "See that fat fellow with the badge and the steam coming out of his ears? That's Sheriff Fisk. Payoff Fisk, I like to call him." He waved. "Sheriff!"

Fisk approached, a Rottweiler who'd gone without his breakfast. "Rosen," he snarled. "You have some gall, being here."

"And this woman with equal gall is Ms. Manfreda, my trusty associate. She's a trial attorney, so watch what you say. She gets real mean when provoked."

Manny studied the nails on her left hand. "Charmed."

"Ms. Manfreda and I are upset," Jake said. "Last time we were in Turner, you were downright ungracious. Knew we were there before I called you—probably the night watchman saw us at the hospital and alerted you. You refused to see us or even listen to what I had to say. Demanded we get out of town. But we're forgiving folk." He marched to within a foot of Fisk and stared into his eyes. "You can stay in Turner; it's welcome to you. And you won't go to jail like you should. But you'll resign as sheriff as of this instant, you'll sever all ties with Reynolds Construction and contribute to Baxter Community Hospital whatever moneys you accrued during that relationship, and you'll issue a public apology to the citizens you used to serve." He took Manny's arm. "Come, Ms. Manfreda. You're averse to maggots, I know, and I don't want you exposed any more than necessary." He turned back to Fisk. "I have complete documentation on all your dealings with Reynolds. So not a peep out of you. We're straight, right? We understand each other, don't we, Fisk?"

If Fisk were a balloon, all the air would go out of him. But he's just as full of himself as ever. He staggered off, muttering, to join the others at the edge of the field.

"You were magnificent," Manny told Jake. "It was the neatest evisceration I've seen since we shared that autopsy room."

Marge Crespy, noticing them, blew them a kiss. A shout arose from the far side of the field, and a trooper ran toward them. "I found something!"

Jake and Manny hurried over. It was a bone. "A tibia," Jake breathed. "And this one's from a different part of the field." He gazed in wonder at the dirt-covered object in the trooper's hand. "There *are* other bodies, Manny, and we're going to find them. Every family has the right to know what happened to their loved one."

She remembered his enthusiasm the first time she saw him, jumping from the helicopter to look at Terrell's body. The same intensity was in him now, electric and dynamic and—there was no other way to describe this dear cutter-up of corpses—full of life.

"If by *we* you mean you, me, and Mycroft, you're right," she promised. "Even if it takes a lifetime."

ACKNOWLEDGMENTS

We would like to take this opportunity to thank the many people without whom Manny and Jake would not have been born. Our dear friends Haskell and Kay Pitluck, who read and reread every draft; our assistant, Patricia Hulbert, and her family, Todd, TJ, Amanda, and Christina (she's not just our assistant, she and her family are our family, too!), who has shepherded us through our courtship, our marriage, and now this project; Sonny Mehta, our publisher, who supported us from the inception; Leigh Feldman, literary agent, dear friend, and muse; Jordan Pavlin, editor, and believer, who gave us the courage and strength to persevere; the brilliant Alfred A. Knopf team, including Paul Bogaards, Gabrielle Brooks, Nicholas Latimer, Erinn Hartman, Sarah Gelman, Farah Miller, Elizabeth Schraft, Anne-Lise Spitzer, and Janet Baker; Linda Fairstein and husband Justin Feldman, for their encouragement, suggestions, and friendship; Dev Chatillon and Barbara Pederson, our lawyers (Manny loves lawyers); Sondra Elkins, who has fought mightily to keep our records accurate; Clay and Silvia McBride, a wonderful husband and wife photographer and make-up artist team; Colin Lively, hair colorist extraordinaire; Pilar and Paul Conceicao, Mycroft's stepparents; Maria Lago, our second mother; Lois R. Densky-Wolff at the University of Medicine and Dentistry of New Jersey Libraries, Special Collections; Anthony Lento, Linda Savino, and all of our friends at Schneider-Nelson Porsche-Audi, for answering every question imaginable about cars; Nancy Martin and Eugene Melody of Martin Melody, Attorneys at Law, where Linda is

ACKNOWLEDGMENTS

Of Counsel; Peter Bogdanovich, who has delightfully helped educate us in the ways of authorship; and Michael Greenfield, for his encouragement and insight. We also thank the FBI and the CIA for so promptly answering our FOIA requests; but most important, we thank the New York State Police—especially forensic dentist Dr. Lowell Levine—who are in the forefront of forensic science.

We thank our children—we love you all so much—for their suggestions and encouragement: Trissa, Lindsey, Sarah, and Christopher, their families and our grandchildren; they are our past, our present, and our future. And finally, of course, we thank Mycroft, our red-headed poodle dog-son, who made all of this possible (but that's another story)!

A NOTE ABOUT THE AUTHORS

Michael Baden, M.D., is one of this country's leading forensic experts. He has overseen cases ranging from the death of John Belushi to the examination of the remains of Tsar Nicholas II, and he has served as an expert witness in countless criminal cases, including the trials of Claus von Bulow and O. J. Simpson. He has been a consulting forensic pathologist to the U.S. State Department, the FBI, and the Russian government, as well as a visiting professor at John Jay College of Criminal Justice and Albert Einstein School of Medicine.

Linda Kenney has won dozens of civil rights lawsuits and has appeared as a legal analyst on Court TV, CNN, and MSNBC. They live in New York City with their dog, Mycroft.

A NOTE ON THE TYPE

This book was set in Janson, a typeface long thought to have been made by the Dutchman Anton Janson, who was a practicing type-founder in Leipzig during the years 1668–1687. However, it has been conclusively demonstrated that these types are actually the work of Nicholas Kis (1650–1702), a Hungarian, who most probably learned his trade from the master Dutch typefounder Dirk Voskens. The type is an excellent example of the influential and sturdy Dutch types that prevailed in England up to the time William Caslon (1692–1766) developed his own incomparable designs from them.

Composed by Creative Graphics, Allentown, Pennsylvania

Printed and bound by Berryville Graphics,

Berryville, Virginia

Designed by Robert C. Olsson